OUTLAW'S QUARRY

OUTLAW'S QUARRY

•

S.J. Stewart

AVALON BOOKS
NEW YORK

Published by Thomas Bouregy & Co., Inc.
160 Madison Avenue, New York, NY 10016

PRINTED IN THE UNITED STATES OF AMERICA
ON ACID-FREE PAPER
BY HADDON CRAFTSMEN, BLOOMSBURG, PENNSYLVANIA

To my lovely granddaughters,
Lacey and Abigail

Chapter One

Shad Wakefield struggled to open his eyes and remember what had happened. His head throbbed and
blood trickled down one side of his face. Beneath him,
he felt the cold unyielding ground. He was surrounded
by darkness. Overhead, the moon looked like a milky
gemstone from a woman's ring, and he was able to
pick out the dipperlike constellation of Ursa Major.
He was just starting to push himself up on one elbow
when he heard the sound of approaching horses. A
half-conscious memory warned him to stay hidden.
When the riders reined up so close that he could smell
horse flesh, he had to choke back anger, for he suddenly remembered everything.

"We can't track Wakefield in the dark," complained
a squeaky voice that belonged to one of Rumbaugh's
outfit.

"I'm afraid he's right, Boss," said another.

Shad held his breath and groped for his Colt revolver, relieved to find that it was still at his side.

"We can't let him get away," said a voice that he recognized as belonging to Rumbaugh. "That two-bit saddle tramp knows too much. If he can get the right people to listen, we'll have more trouble than we can handle."

"Well, if you can follow his tracks in the dark, you can do better than me."

The man seemed to have gotten through to Rumbaugh, for he reluctantly agreed to call off the hunt.

"We'll camp here tonight and get an early start in the morning."

This wasn't what Shad wanted to hear, for all that separated him from the gang was the width of a boulder. He had no horse, and he was wounded.

"I tell you, I think I winged him," insisted Squeaky Voice. "He's not going to get far."

"We'll see," said Rumbaugh. "But if you'd done your job right in the first place we wouldn't have to be up here lookin' for his tracks."

Shad remained quiet, not daring to move a muscle lest he give himself away. He listened as they went off a short distance and ground-tethered their horses. Then he heard them gathering wood to build a campfire. Soon the aroma of hot coffee drifted over to where he lay hidden. He yearned for even a few swallows, for it was all he could do to keep his teeth from chattering. After nightfall, it was cold on the mountain.

He lay huddled in the darkness, his head aching

from the wound. Rumbaugh's outfit ate, and then they talked among themselves for awhile. Shad thought he'd freeze to death before they finally climbed into their bedrolls. Still he waited, allowing time for them to fall asleep. When he heard them snoring, he got to his knees and crawled away. The going was difficult on muscles long unused. Besides that, his head still ached and his body was bruised.

He had no idea where the sorrel had gone after he'd fallen from its saddle, but it carried his canteen, a meager food supply, and his bedroll. It was also his means of getting off the mountain and across the plains to Judge Madison's place. He was aware that if he had to go all the way on foot his prospects were grim. But this was something he couldn't let himself think about. Not yet.

Keeping low, he quietly, painstakingly made his way up the mountainside in the darkness. Rumbaugh had been right. If Shad got the chance to tell about the shootings, Rumbaugh's neck would be in a noose. Old man Craddock had friends, and so did Charlie Pickett.

All around him the pines, spruces, and aspens grew thick. He'd changed to an upright position, but he had to stop from time to time to let his head clear before pressing on. He had no hope that Rumbaugh would give up the chase and turn back. Shad was a witness to Craddock's murder, not to mention Charlie's.

Shad and Charlie had been looking for some stray cattle when they saw the shooting from a nearby rise. It was well known that Rumbaugh wanted Craddock's land, along with the water that went with it. But the ranchers had been intimidated by Rumbaugh. They'd never stand up to him and demand justice unless there was a witness to what he'd done. He was too powerful and much too dangerous. Rumbaugh was well aware of this. When he'd spotted Shad and Charlie on that rise, he'd ordered them killed. A bullet had downed Charlie, and another had wounded Shad. He had no doubt that Rumbaugh intended to finish the job come morning.

With his strength almost exhausted, Shad reached a shelf that was leveled off and filled with a grove of aspens. Here he paused to rest. A stream of water, cold as the snow-melt that it was, ran through the grove. He heard it, and smelled the wetness of it, before he actually saw it in the dappled moonlight. He knelt there on the bank and quenched his thirst. When he finished, he washed his face and injured head. Then with his fingertips he gently explored the wound. Although it had bled a little and hurt a lot, it was only a graze. He'd been lucky and he knew it.

As he started to get up, he heard the sound of a snapping twig somewhere back in the darkness. His hand went for the gun at his side, and he swiveled around to face the threat. A horse whinnied softly, and the sorrel stepped into the clearing. Shad almost laughed with relief.

"Well, I'm sure glad to see you, old pal," he said, grasping the reins and giving the horse a pat on the neck.

He figured the sorrel must have found this place and then stayed here because of the water. A quick check reassured him that everything in the saddlebags was still intact. Even better, his rifle was in its scabbard.

"We'd better get ourselves away from here *pronto*," he said.

He climbed into the saddle and urged the horse into the water. He intended to make it as hard as he could for Rumbaugh and his outfit to track him. No doubt at dawn they'd find where he'd fallen, and it wouldn't take them long to pick up his trail. But now his chances were a whole lot better. He was mounted and he had a good head start.

His first thought had been to go back to the Circle C, where he worked. But Rumbaugh would expect him to do this. No doubt he'd send a man with a rifle to wait for Shad and pick him off from cover. His second thought was Trinidad. The killers wouldn't be expecting this. At Trinidad he could let Judge Madison know what had happened. Judge Madison could then pass that information on to a federal marshal. Once this was done, Shad vowed to find a way to confront Rumbaugh on more equal terms.

After keeping the sorrel in the cold water as long as he dared, he rode out of the stream and began to climb higher, leaving the shelf behind. He needed to find his way southward, so that when he left the cover of the mountain wilderness, he would be far from where the outlaws had followed him from the plains. He figured it would buy him some time if they believed he was going all the way over to the other side. So he continued on as if this were his plan, until he spotted a faint trail in the moonlight. It appeared to follow the curve of the mountain toward the south. He nudged the sorrel onto the narrow route, and proceeded to ride into the unknown. He had no idea if the trail had been made by Kiowas or Utes, or perhaps by some other, much older tribe. He also had no idea how far it would take him.

By the time it was daylight, he should have felt sick and bone-tired, but he'd gotten his second wind. Not only that, his head was clear and the pain had eased. During the night, he'd put a lot of distance between himself and his pursuers. Still, he had to keep moving, and he had to be careful.

At twenty-two, his youth was in his favor, and all those hard days on the range had made him strong. He was taller than average, like his father had been, and well-muscled, and lean. He was stubborn like his father as well. He figured that maybe a stubborn streak was a good thing. It kept you going after everyone else had quit.

No doubt, Rumbaugh and his gang had crawled out of their beds by this time and were looking for him. But he'd done his best to make his trail a hard one to follow.

The sun was moving leisurely across a nearly cloudless blue sky, and the forest was alive with birdsong. Under other circumstances his surroundings would have brought pleasure. But his grief and anger were too great to allow him any peace. Not only that, he hated to be running away. He preferred to fight an enemy face to face, but for now he was reduced to being Rumbaugh's quarry.

At intervals he paused to listen for the sounds of horses or voices. Each time, he heard only the natural noises of the wilderness. At last he let himself believe that Rumbaugh might have lost his trail and turned back. The hope was tentative at first, but as time passed it grew stronger.

When morning had turned to afternoon, the old trail began to descend. He calculated that it would bring him off the mountain far and away from where he'd begun his climb. But before he risked the plains where he could be seen for miles, he needed rest. So did the horse.

Shad dismounted and cut pine boughs to make a brushy screen. Behind these he hobbled the sorrel and spread out his bedroll. This done, he managed to eat a cold biscuit and wash it down with water. Then he slept lightly with his rifle across his chest. It was evening when he awoke and continued on his way.

The trail had been descending gently, but now the descent grew steeper as he carefully picked his way down the mountainside in the moonlight. An owl hooted in the distance, causing him concern, for this was often the signal of an unseen enemy. Tonight, though, it was just the night call of an owl.

It was still dark when he left the foothills behind, but the constellations had moved across the sky, and he knew it was only a short time until dawn. He rode hard all day, and before night fell again, he rode into Trinidad.

Because of the Santa Fe trade route the town was thriving. On the outskirts, teamsters were camped, getting ready for the long ordeal of Raton Pass. Shad turned down a side street and made his way to the large adobe house of Judge Harley Madison. He dismounted and started for the door, but before he could get there, a weathered old cowpoke ambled around the corner of the house.

"Why Shadrach Wakefield, as I live and breathe. What brings you off the prairie?"

It was Abe Featherstone, the man who'd been looking out for Judge Madison's interests for years. He was part valet, part bodyguard, and sometimes a caretaker. His hair was a mixture of brown and white, and he had no extra meat on his bones. Most noticeable were his eyes, which looked like the soulful, droopy eyes of an old bloodhound.

"It's good to see you, Abe," Shad said, offering his hand. "You're looking spry as ever."

Abe glanced at his wounded head, for in spite of his hat, the clotted blood was visible.

"Well, I can't say that you're lookin' too spry right now. It appears that you tried to dodge a bullet and didn't quite get the job done."

"That's one of the things I need to talk to the Judge about. Is he around?"

Abe looked regretful.

"No, Shad, he ain't. The Judge had to go up to Denver City on business and he didn't know when he'd get back. He's been gone a month now."

Shad felt like he'd had the air knocked out of him. He'd been depending on the Judge to help him deal with Rumbaugh and his outfit in a legal way.

"Why don't you tell me what the trouble is," Abe urged. "Maybe there's something I can do to help. Come on to my place and rest yourself for a spell."

Abe's place was a small adobe dwelling at the back of Judge Madison's extensive town property. Inside the low-ceilinged room, he seated himself at the table.

"I don't like to heat up the place building a fire to make coffee," Abe said. "This time of year I do all the cooking outside over a fire, or in that adobe oven. Once that thing heats up, it just don't want to cool down."

"That's okay," Shad said.

Abe went to a shelf and took down a bottle of whiskey. He poured some of it into a tin cup and handed it to Shad.

"The way you're lookin' right now, maybe you need this kind of drink worse, anyway. I keep this here bottle on hand for medicinal purposes. The Judge don't hold too much with drinkin'."

Shad took the proffered cup and nodded.

"I remember. He has his own ways."

"That he does, son. That he does."

Shad downed the whiskey and hoped its medicinal qualities, if any, would work.

"Now, while I clean and dress that wound of yours, you'd better tell me what's going on."

While Abe worked on his head, Shad told how he and Charlie had witnessed the killing of old man Craddock, and about Charlie's murder. He told of his escape to the mountain and of Rumbaugh's pursuit.

When Abe finished dressing his wound, he went over and sat down at the table across from him.

"You know, we've been hearing stories about that Rumbaugh fellow for some time now. He's been walkin' over a lot of folks, from all accounts."

"That's the truth for sure. What we need, Abe, is a law officer and a posse. He's got a bunch of hardcases working for him, and that place of his is a veritable fortress. Not to mention that he's got a lot of people scared, and for good reason."

"You still workin' for Luke Crane?"

"Yeah. He'll be wondering what happened to me and Charlie. Although they may have found what's left of Charlie by now."

"It's too bad to lose a good man," Abe sympathized.

Shad didn't want to think about it any more. At least not right then.

"Did the Judge mention where he'd be staying in Denver City?" he asked, as much for information as to change the subject.

"At the house of a friend of his named Neeley. Andrew Neeley. They've knowed each other from way back, and I reckon the Judge and him have a good time remembering the past together."

Shad set the empty cup on the table and got up.

"I think I'll telegraph him and let him know what's going on. Guess there's not much he can do from Denver City, though."

Abe cleared his throat.

"A person might be surprised what the Judge can do when he sets his mind to it."

Shad didn't contradict him. Abe was as loyal as a man could be, and in his own book, loyalty was a fine quality.

"Well then, I'd better get down to the telegraph office before it closes. If you could let me put my feet under your table for supper, I'd be much obliged."

"I'd be disappointed if you didn't, son. You just come right on back here as soon as you get that message sent."

The telegrapher did a double-take when Shad walked into the office just as he was getting ready to close. In spite of the fresh bandage that Abe had applied, he must have looked like the loser in a serious saloon fight.

"I need to send a message to Denver City," he said.

The telegrapher shoved a pad of paper and the nubbin of a pencil toward him.

"Better make it fast," he warned, "for it's time I was closin' up."

Shad hastily scribbled a note under the Judge's name and Denver City address. Beneath, he signed it simply "Shad" and placed a gold piece beside it.

"Here you go," he said.

The telegrapher, who'd been hovering with a scowl on his face, scooped up the money and took the note. After scanning it, his manner underwent a change.

"I'll get this right out, Sir," he said with a tone of respect in his voice. "I didn't realize it was so important. Just a moment and I'll get your change."

Shad was amused, but tried not to show it.

"Forget it. I put you out by keeping you past your closing time."

"Thank you, Sir," the telegrapher said and hurried to get the message dispatched.

Shad noted that the combination of gold and the Judge's name had brought him instant respect, something his disheveled appearance and messy head wound had failed to do.

With his task completed, he left the office and made his way back to Abe's house. He was hungry after two hard nights and days with skimpy rations, and he remembered that Abe was a better-than-average cook.

Following a meal of fried venison, boiled greens, and stewed apples, he accompanied Abe as the older man made his round of the Judge's property, which was one of his duties. Abe asked him what he planned to do.

"You know you're welcome to stay here, son, and wait for the Judge to return."

"I can't, Abe, although I'm obliged for the invitation. I've got to get back and let folks know what happened to Charlie and to Ben Craddock."

"Well, I can't let you go back there alone. If you're plannin' on pulling out in the morning, I'll be ready to ride along."

Shad was grateful for the offer but he protested. "What about looking out for the Judge's place, and taking care of his interests?"

"Oh, Griego will be glad to do it. He lives just across the way, and I recollect that he owes the Judge a favor or two."

"Then I'd be pleased to have your company. But I should warn you that Rumbaugh and his outfit are dangerous. If they see you with me, they'll figure you know about the killings too. That makes you a target."

"Son, I've been around the block a few times, and I've seen a lot of Rumbaugh's kind. Don't worry that I'm stumbling blind into a bad situation. Truth is, I've been sitting around here on my backside too long. It's not like the old days used to be. I expect it'll do me good to get out of town for a spell."

"Then we'll ride at dawn."

Abe stopped as if he'd had a sudden thought.

"Shad, I hope you don't mind if another fellow goes along with us."

"Who'd you have in mind?"

"A young fellow named Mc Nary."

"Does he know Rumbaugh?"

"You might say that. He used to work for him."

Shad wasn't sure he'd heard right.

"What did you say?"

"Mc Nary used to be one of Rumbaugh's hired hands, but Rumbaugh pistol-whipped him because he disobeyed an order to beat up a kid whose father had been troublesome."

"Sounds like Mc Nary might have a sense of honor."

"Maybe," said Abe. "At least he nurses a deep hatred for Rumbaugh, and he knows Rumbaugh's stronghold inside out. That might turn out to be useful to us."

Shad had to agree.

"Can he be ready to ride at first light?"

"I'll tell him," said Abe. "Now you'd better get some rest. You, sure as sin, look like you could use it."

Shad figured he was right about that, and a little rest was known to be good medicine. He walked back to the house alone while Abe went to talk to Mc Nary. He spread his bedroll on the floor and was soon asleep.

Before daylight, he crawled out when he smelled breakfast cooking. Abe had stirred up a meal of bacon, eggs, biscuits, and coffee.

"Good mornin', Shad," he said. "I thought we both could use some fortification. Fill your plate whenever you're ready."

"I'll just be a minute."

Shad stepped outside to the pump, where he splashed water on his face. It was still dark, and the cold air shocked him to alertness as much as the cold water. Shivering and wide awake, he went back to eat breakfast.

"Where's this Mc Nary fellow who's supposed to be here by now?" he asked before forking in a mouthful of bacon.

"He wasn't supposed to arrive until first light. He'll be here."

It turned out Abe was right, for just as the first hint of pink showed in the eastern sky, Mc Nary rode up, leading a spare mount. He didn't look much older than Shad. In appearance, though, he was shorter and stockier. His nose had been broken, and when he walked over to where they were waiting, he had a noticeable limp. Abe made the introduction.

"This here is Shadrach Wakefield that I was telling you about."

"Howdy. I'm Dan Mc Nary, the man who hates Jake Rumbaugh more than anyone else in Colorado does, and that's goin' some, for Rumbaugh is real good at making enemies."

"Glad to have you along," said Shad. "But I want something understood before we start. I'm the boss. What I say goes."

There was a pause before Mc Nary answered.

"Sure," he agreed without sounding altogether sincere. "Now, let's get out of here and go outlaw hunting."

"As far as I'm concerned, you're the boss, Shadrach," said Abe, calling him once more by his formal name.

With that assurance, Shad mounted the sorrel and rode out of Trinidad with the others. The teamsters on the outskirts of town were just waking. Their oxen had been herded into a makeshift corral, and the pungent odor of their droppings tainted the early morning air.

"How long do you think they'll stay?" he asked Abe.

"Oh, I expect they'll be moving out today. Most likely it'll take them a week to get through the pass, and they still have a ways to go after that."

Shad had great respect for the men who hauled cargo all the way from Missouri under less than ideal conditions. But the rewards were usually ample enough to compensate for the hard work and the risks they took.

With the large mesa that overlooked Trinidad behind them, Shad, Abe, and Mc Nary headed north for the plains. Shad was glad to have the two men with him; there were times when a man shouldn't have to ride alone, and this was one of them.

When they stopped to eat and rest the horses, he decided to question Mc Nary. "Nobody seems to know where Rumbaugh came from, or how he got started," he said. "Do you know anything about the man?"

"More than I want to," Mc Nary replied. "He bragged a time or two about how he'd escaped the hangman's noose back East. Once, when he was liquored up, he talked about his old man. Said he was some big shot who expected a lot from his sons. Apparently Rumbaugh was the black sheep of his family. Seems like he was born with a mean streak and never amounted to nothing. He started moving west to escape the law. Eventually, he got to Colorado. Once he arrived, he came down with a bad case of greed and started walkin' all over people."

"Maybe we should wait until the Judge gets back and charge his bailiwick with a well-armed posse," Abe suggested.

"Wouldn't do any good," warned Mc Nary. "Rumbaugh is prepared for something like that. He has the place heavily fortified and he's hired plenty of men at top dollar to defend it. A citizen posse wouldn't stand a chance."

While Shad hadn't gotten close to Rumbaugh's place, he wasn't surprised at Mc Nary's evaluation. In fact, he'd have been surprised if it had been otherwise.

"We'll go on," he said. "I need to tell my boss what happened to Charlie. Then maybe we can scout out the stronghold, and figure out Rumbaugh's weaknesses."

"Rumbaugh doesn't have any weaknesses," Mc Nary said. "He's made sure of that. There were times when I used to think that he was so full of himself that he believed he could take over the whole bloomin' Territory."

Shad had no doubt that Mc Nary was real close to the truth.

The three men remounted and rode in companionable silence. Before the seemingly endless plains got firmly established, there were a few towering mesas, along with modest rises and dips in the landscape. Still, it was possible to see for a great distance in most places. To their left rose the Spanish Peaks which dominated the landscape. But Luke Crane's Circle C Ranch lay to the north, and this was where Shad needed to go first. For the past couple of years, he'd ridden for Crane's outfit, and so had Charlie.

It was evening when they crossed the Apishapa River and found a place to make camp. Shad noticed that Mc Nary took the time to check his guns. While the man wore only one Colt, which he strapped down like a gunslinger would wear it, he stowed another exactly like it in his saddlebag. He also kept a Win-

chester rifle in a scabbard. Whatever else Mc Nary
might be, he was a wary, well-armed ally.

They'd been careful to camp where they could build
a small fire in a draw. It would be impossible for anyone to see it unless he was right on top of them. Still,
they sat in the shadows some distance away from the
flames. Shad couldn't discount the possibility that
Rumbaugh had either picked up his trail, or else as-
sumed that his quarry would head to Trinidad for help.
It was likely that he'd posted men to watch for Shad's
return.

After the others had turned in, he stayed awake for
a time and tried to think like a power-hungry outlaw.
If he were in Rumbaugh's boots, he'd figure that his
enemies would either have to be killed or discredited.
Those were the only two choices, and Jake Rumbaugh
seemed to favor killing.

Shad noticed that Abe had dropped off to sleep, for
the man was snoring like all get out. Mc Nary appeared to be asleep too, which left Shad to stand
watch. The job was one he'd taken on himself, for the
others believed that their whereabouts were unknown
to Rumbaugh. He stayed back in the shadows and
fought the drowsiness that threatened to overpower
him. He was barely winning the battle, when a bullet
smashed into the coffeepot. The dregs of the pot
spilled onto the dying embers, causing steam to hiss
upward. Shad was instantly on his belly, firing into the
darkness. Abe and Mc Nary quickly joined in.

From the positions of the gunfire, Shad could tell
that four of Rumbaugh's men were attacking. He fired

into the darkness, and was rewarded by a cry of pain as one of the outlaws took a hit. Then the firing tapered off. Now, only two guns were keeping them pinned. With just one attacker down, Shad had to make an assumption that he didn't like. In all probability, one of the outlaws was moving into place to attack them from behind. He rolled over on his back and spotted a shadowy figure raising up to draw a bead on Abe. Shad fired, and his bullet hit home. The attacker's gun discharged harmlessly in the air as he fell.

Only two of them were left, and the outlaws didn't appear to like the odds. The firing stopped. Before Shad could reload his pistol, he heard the sound of retreating horses.

"That was a close call," said Abe after they were gone. "A fellow can't get a good night's sleep around here. Guess I'd better check on the ones we dropped, just to make sure."

"Be careful," Mc Nary warned.

"You can bet on it," Abe replied.

Since they were betting, Shad was willing to bet six months' pay that this wouldn't be the last close call they'd have. Rumbaugh hadn't wasted any time sending his men out looking. He wanted Shad dead in the worst way, and he wasn't the kind to give up.

Chapter Two

They packed up and rode out before dawn. The attack had left them all on edge and jumping at shadows. Shad figured it would take awhile for Rumbaugh's men to get back and report to their boss, and this would give him and his partners some time. With luck they'd make it to the safety of the Circle C before another sunset.

But he had to consider that a gunman might have been posted to watch the ranch with orders to shoot him when he approached. Shad decided it would be wise to wait until dark before they rode in.

"I think you're doing the right thing," Abe agreed when Shad voiced his concern. "A man can't be too careful."

"Especially where Jake Rumbaugh is concerned," Mc Nary agreed.

They stopped a considerable distance away from the ranch buildings, where they waited in a wash until after dark. When they did ride in, Shad was surprised at what they found. The entire place appeared to be deserted.

"The boss must have everybody out looking for the missing cattle that me and Charlie were hunting."

Still, it seemed strange to him that Crane would give such an order to his men. There were other things that needed to be considered. The livestock, for instance, as well as keeping an eye on the place. While the number of head they'd been missing was significant, that number didn't warrant an all-out search by the entire outfit.

"We'll go on in and make ourselves at home," he said. "The horses could use some oats, and I think they've earned 'em."

They dismounted and headed for the barn with Shad in the lead. He stepped inside and met Tex Hubble on his way out with a lantern in one hand.

"Howdy," he said, seeing the look of surprise on Tex's face in the lantern light.

The next thing he knew, Tex had drawn his pistol and was pointing it straight at Shad's midsection. The look of surprise had turned to one of hatred.

"You no-account murderer," Tex accused. "You sure have your nerve coming back here after gunning down Charlie the way you did, just because he tried to stop you from shooting old man Craddock."

It was Shad's turn to show surprise.

"Now, Wakefield, you're going to die like you deserve," said Tex, moving the barrel of the gun slightly so it was aiming right at Shad's heart.

"Hold it," Abe ordered as he stepped in front of the opening with his gun drawn, letting himself be seen by Tex for the first time.

Tex froze.

"I didn't kill Charlie," Shad assured him.

"You lyin' scum. There was witnesses. Plenty of 'em."

"And they all work for Jake Rumbaugh," Mc Nary said as he made his own appearance.

"So what?" said Tex. "A witness is a witness."

"Not by a long shot," Shad contradicted. "It was Rumbaugh that killed Ben Craddock, and it was me and Charlie that were the witnesses. Rumbaugh and his men saw us and they came after us. Rumbaugh shot Charlie, and one of his men grazed my head with a bullet. The results you can plainly see."

He pointed to the bandage.

"Besides," he went on, "it was Rumbaugh who had a reason to kill Craddock, not me. Everyone knows that he wants Craddock's ranch and the water that goes with it. He's been trying for a long time to run him off, but the old man was tough and stubborn. He refused to go, so Rumbaugh and his men murdered him. Charlie and me saw it plain as day from that rise just north of his house."

"And if you'd like to place a little bet," Mc Nary said, "I'll bet you a two dollar gold piece that some of Rumbaugh's gun hands are at the Craddock place right now. I'll bet they won't let you come within shoutin' distance. Besides, if Rumbaugh wasn't there at the killing, how could he claim to know Charlie had seen Shad kill Craddock?"

Shad could see they were getting through to Tex. He'd started thinking for himself again. It looked like all the others had jumped onto Jake Rumbaugh's bandwagon without an ounce of proof or a trace of loyalty to Shad.

"You've been real lucky, Wakefield," his former friend told him. "The boss has just about every hand out combing the Territory for you. When they found you, they were going to string you up from the nearest tree."

Shad felt ice cold inside. He'd ridden for the brand for more than two years. All during that time, he'd been as loyal to Luke Crane as a man could be, and he'd considered the other cowhands to be his friends. Now, all of them had turned on him, based on the transparent lies of a man they all knew to be a scoundrel. It seemed that every one of Crane's hands had been eager to attend Shad's necktie party, not to mention Crane himself, regardless of the law. Without giving him a chance to speak in his own defense, they were ready to see him die at the end of a rope. It sickened him. But that was human nature, he told himself. Only it wasn't the nature of Abe Featherstone, or Harley Madison, or Dunham Wakefield, the father who'd raised him. It wasn't his own nature, either. He trusted his friends. If a man didn't trust in friends, what was the point in having them? The men he'd ridden with for so long weren't friends after all, and

Luke Crane hadn't returned the loyalty that Shad had given him so freely.

"You can understand why I'm not waiting around," he said, "so I'd be obliged, Tex, if you'd give your boss a message when you see him. Tell him I quit. He can send the wages that he owes me to Judge Harley Madison at Trinidad, if he's honest enough to pay 'em. I regret that I spent two years workin' for a man who'd hang me without a trial on the obvious lie of a thief and a killer."

"I'll tell him," Tex said. "I'll tell him what you said about Rumbaugh being the one who shot Charlie too, but I don't think that him and the others will believe it. Once the boss makes up his mind, he sticks with it."

That was true enough. Not only was Luke Crane a shallow thinker, but he was downright bullheaded.

"Look here, Tex, you know that Charlie was as close to me as a brother. I had no reason to kill him. Rumbaugh had a big reason to kill Craddock, and because we saw it, Rumbaugh had a big reason to kill us too. He succeeded with Charlie. He almost succeeded with me. Judge Madison knows all about it, and anyone with a lick of common sense could figure it out for himself."

Mc Nary spoke from the doorway where he was keeping watch.

"Rumbaugh's a wanted man. He came to Colorado Territory to escape the hangman's noose back East."

Tex looked shamefaced.

"I'm sorry for what I thought about you, Shad. I'll

talk to the others and convince 'em, somehow, that you're okay."

"Obliged," Shad told him, thinking that an ounce of trust in the first place would have been worth a whole lot more.

While Abe kept a look-out and Mc Nary fed and watered the horses, Shad walked over to the corral with Tex, who still held the lantern. Often when he was working he drew his mounts from the remuda, but the sorrel was his own, as was the line-back dun in the corral.

"I'm takin' my horse," he said.

"Sure," Tex agreed and watched as Shad fetched him from the enclosure.

Abe and Mc Nary had brought spare horses with them. Now, with the dun in his possession as well as the sorrel, he felt a lot better.

"Where is it that you're headed?" Tex asked as he watched Shad switch his saddle from the sorrel to the dun.

"Now, that's a piece of information that I don't care to share with a lynch mob."

It gave him a measure of satisfaction to see Tex wince.

"Well, Shad, just so you'll know, the boss and the rest of 'em took out toward the mountains. That's where Rumbaugh said you ran after you killed Charlie."

"That's where I ran after Rumbaugh killed Charlie," Shad amended. "Nice of Rumbaugh to get my boss and my so-called friends to do his dirty work for him."

"Are you ready to go?" Mc Nary asked, leading the other horses from the barn.

"You bet. I want to get out of here *pronto*."

"Just hold on a minute," Abe said. "You'll have to forgive me for being a man with a suspicious nature, Tex. But just in case you're not sincere in your conversion, and just so you won't shoot us the minute our backs are turned, I'll take that revolver of yours. When we're out a ways, I'll lay it on the ground and you can fetch it come daylight."

Tex started to protest but thought better of it. Instead, he stood quietly waiting while they rode away. True to his word, Abe stopped and laid the pistol on the ground before they went on.

"What's your plan now?" Mc Nary asked.

Shad had been thinking about that ever since the first plan, that of enlisting the men of the Circle C, fell through.

"We still need help if we're to put a stop to Rumbaugh and his gang. We'll just have to get it elsewhere."

"And how do you plan to do that?" Abe questioned.

"I've been doing some thinking. There's a lot of folks around here that Rumbaugh's stepped on pretty hard. The Circle C is large and powerful, so he's left it alone. That's the main reason why Crane's feelings about him were neutral enough that he was willing to believe Rumbaugh's story. But there are plenty of others who know him for what he is. I think, given the chance, they'd ride with us."

"Could be you're right," the older man agreed. "Where do you think we should start?"

"The Kaminski place."

The A Bar K was a much smaller operation than the Circle C. Augustyn Kaminski managed to pay only enough hands to keep it going, and Rumbaugh considered it easy pickings. He'd needled the Polish immigrant by calling him names in front of others, and by threatening to burn his house. There had also been accounts of Rumbaugh's hands harassing the men who rode for him. But Kaminski was determined to stay.

The rancher's house was only an hour's ride from where they were. When they got within hailing distance, Shad gave a shout. The house was so still that it looked deserted. Then in the moonlight, he saw the door ease open a little.

"Who's out there?" came the heavily accented voice of Kaminski.

"It's Shad Wakefield and a couple of friends. We're here to talk to you about Jake Rumbaugh."

There was a moment's hesitation.

"Then come on in," he said.

By the time they got to the door, a coal oil lamp had been lit, and Kaminski had donned his trousers over his nightshirt. He was a big man, muscled from hard work, with a face reddened by the sun.

"I'm surprised to see that you're still alive, Shad Wakefield, but I'm most pleased about it. A fellow stopped by here yesterday and said you were wanted for two murders. The trouble was, I couldn't see a reason for you killing either one, and I've got no use at all for the man who started the rumor."

He offered his hand and Shad shook it before introducing Abe and Mc Nary.

"I suppose you know," Kaminski said, "that Crane and his boys are out beating the bushes for you, and so is the Rumbaugh outfit. They've got a rope with your name on it. At least that's what the fellow told me who was spreading the word."

"How can the Circle C bunch be such idiots!" Mc Nary exclaimed. "I hope the rest of the people don't think like they do."

"Not all of them do," Kaminski said. "Not the ones that Rumbaugh's been pushing around. A lot of us were worried about old Ben Craddock, for Rumbaugh was running off his cattle and his hands, and leaving him wide open for what happened."

"Are any of you willing to do something about it?" Shad asked him.

"As long as it doesn't include suicide, I'm willing. Just what is it that you have in mind to do?"

"We've got to use force since it's all Rumbaugh understands. We need to form our own posse and put an end to the killing, rustling, and land-grabbing."

They all found places in the small room to sit down. Shad glanced at Kaminski. In the lamp light, his broad, ruddy face appeared thoughtful.

"So Wakefield, what you're talking about is raising a band of vigilantes." The final word came out with a hint of distaste.

"If that's what you want to call 'em. When the law

can't handle the likes of Rumbaugh, it's left to citizen vigilantes to do it. If we don't do something to stop him, there's going to be more killings, and he's going to take over and run the place like a land baron."

"You've got a point, but I can't see your boss sticking his neck out. Crane looks after himself and nobody else. He can't see that Rumbaugh's going after the easier targets first and the Circle C will come later. In fact, it appears that he's actually allied himself with that outlaw in order to lynch one of his own men."

Shad felt another wave of anger, but it wasn't toward Kaminski, who was simply pointing out a fact. His anger was for the disloyalty and stupidity of Luke Crane.

"Crane's not my boss anymore," Shad told him. "We don't need him, anyway. What we do need is some men who are smart enough to know what they're doing, and who have the guts to carry it through."

Abe, who'd been silent, cleared his throat."

"Given up on the Judge, have you, son?"

"I haven't given up, but what can he do? He's not here with either military or civilian forces. He can't even add his own rifle to the cause."

"That's a fact," Mc Nary said. "We've got to handle this ourselves."

"Then you'll want to start with Joe and Cory Beale, Hiram Loftis, and the Osborns," Kaminski advised.

Shad knew the Osborn brothers, and he'd met Cory Beale. But Cory's uncle and Loftis were strangers to him.

"Kaminski, if you're acquainted with Loftis, it

might be better if you talked to him," he said. "I'll ride over and see the Osborns."

"If you like," Mc Nary said, "I'll speak to Cory Beale. His uncle's not too sociable, but Cory's okay."

"Good idea," Shad agreed.

"Then why don't I make you fellows something to eat?" Kaminski offered. "After you've got your bellies full, you can get some rest. We can get an early start come daylight."

Shad glanced over at Abe, who hadn't said a word.

"Why don't you stay here and keep an eye on the place?" he suggested.

"No need," said Kaminski. "Scruggs and Henley can do that. That way your friend can ride along with you. The way things are, you ought not be out there alone."

It turned out that Kaminski's hands were camped out in the barn. Had he given a holler, they'd have come running, armed to the teeth.

"A man can't be too cautious," Kaminski explained, as if he'd sensed Shad's thoughts.

He called in Scruggs and Henley and introduced them to the others. Then the big man set to work frying a pan of bacon, along with about a dozen fresh eggs from his chicken coop. Added to that was johnnycake and a pot of strong coffee. It was the best meal Shad had eaten since Trinidad. When he finished, he spread his bedroll outside the door and turned in. And before daylight, he was astride his horse and riding north toward the Osborn place, Abe riding beside him.

"I expect that by this time those two outlaws who

survived the shoot-out will have reported to their boss," Abe said. "Rumbaugh is going to be mad enough to kick a hog barefooted, and he's going to figure that you've headed for home."

Shad started to inform him that the Circle C wasn't his home—not anymore. Then he decided it was better to just let it go.

They kept a look-out for any of Rumbaugh's men who might be out searching for him, and they watched for Circle C hands as well. Luck was with them, for they arrived at the Osborn ranch without incident. Cletus Osborn limped off the front porch and came to meet them. His right leg was tied in splints, and his homely face sported a grin.

"Shad Wakefield, what in the world are you doing here? There's a price on your head, you know."

Neither Kaminski nor Tex had mentioned any reward money. He wondered how much his hide was worth, and asked.

"A hundred and fifty dollars dead or alive, but preferably dead."

The amount staggered him.

"All on just Rumbaugh's word? No evidence. No trial. No nothing."

"That's about the size of it, my friend. Now, why don't you two climb down off them horses and come on in out of the sun."

Shad and Abe dismounted and followed Cletus inside the small house. Shad wondered how Kaminski could be put off by the word "vigilante" when Rumbaugh could put a price on a man's life, just like that, and get away with it.

"What happened to your leg?" Abe asked, pointing to the splints.

"Busted it the other day. A horse fell on me."

"Ouch," Abe commiserated, "that had to hurt."

"Just a mite, but it was my own fault. I'll know better next time."

They settled around the table, and Cletus poured them cups of water that had been cooled outside in the *olla* that hung from a tree limb.

"Where's Slim?" Shad asked. "We'd like to talk to him too."

"He went out to check on the hands. They've been having trouble locating a sizeable portion of the herd."

"That seems to be a common problem around here. That's what Charlie and me were doing when we caught sight of Rumbaugh puttin' a bullet into Ben Craddock."

"So that's how it was."

Shad went on to tell Cletus what had happened and what it was they were planning to do about it.

"Well, it's about time somebody put a stop to this lawlessness," Cletus agreed. "Not that I can be all that much help with this bum leg, but I can sit a horse for sure, and I can still shoot straight. You can bet that Slim will join us, too, and he's a better shot than I am."

"Appreciate it," said Shad as he got up. "Meet us in the draw behind Kaminski's place. In case anybody's watching, I don't want to attract attention by having everyone ride up to the house in plain sight."

"You leavin' already?" Cletus asked.

"Afraid we have to. We've got some things to see about."

"Then be real careful. Some of your old friends might not be friends anymore. Your hide is worth a powerful lot of money."

To Shad, having a bounty put on him like a coyote or a wolf was dehumanizing. Especially since he'd done nothing to deserve it. He despised Rumbaugh as much for that as for anything else he'd done. No two ways about it, he had a score to settle, and after he'd finished, Rumbaugh wouldn't be putting a bounty on anyone else's head. Not ever.

Chapter Three

Shad took the lead. He wasn't in the mood to talk, and Abe respected the silence between them. He was a good man to partner with, as good as Charlie had been. They kept mostly to the low places, staying out of sight as much as possible. Often this wasn't possible and then they took their chances, hoping that none of their enemies would spot them. Overhead the sky was streaked with long wispy clouds, the kind Shad had spent hours watching since his return to Colorado. Sometimes it seemed to him that things were the same as they'd always been, but those feelings were short-lived. The reality was that he'd lost one of his friends to a bullet, and most of the others to a lie. On top of that, his life was in danger of being a short one, with so many out after his hide.

"You know, Shad," said Abe, "you remind me a whole lot of your pa, the way he never backed off from nothin'. There were times when I was convinced that he'd taken leave of his senses, but he always came out all right, except for that last time."

Shad knew about Abe's friendship with his father. When he spoke about "that last time," he meant the time when Dunham Wakefield had been gunned down by the outlaws he'd set out to capture. Abe was with Judge Madison when the Judge had told the thirteen-year-old Shad of his father's death.

"Son, this kind of thing happens sometimes when a man pins on a badge," he'd said. "Taking risks is part of the job, and it's an important job that somebody has to do. Your father was a brave and honorable man. People looked up to him and they respected him. Don't you ever forget that."

In spite of the Judge's intention, his words had been scant comfort. Shad hated the badge that had taken his father away from him. He hated it almost as much as he despised the outlaws who'd gunned Dunham Wakefield down.

"Now, don't you worry about a thing, son, for you're coming home with me," the Judge had told him after the burying.

That afternoon, he had gathered his belongings from the little house that he'd shared with his father and he'd moved in with the Judge. There he stayed, until the day his guardian put him on a wagon that was headed for Missouri.

"I know you can't see it right now, Shad, but this is for the best," the Judge had insisted. "You've got a good mind and you need to get some schooling."

Whenever the Judge made up his mind, that was that. There would be no reprieve.

The journey east was long and arduous. Eventually, he ended up at the house of the Judge's sister in St. Louis, where his arrival coincided with the outbreak of the Civil War. It was a time of unrest, and Shad had too much to see and to think about to be homesick. He'd listened as the city buzzed with news of the activities of Nathaniel Lyon. The red-headed officer had taken his men and raided the armory. Then he'd spirited the weapons across the Mississippi River to Illinois, which was securely Union. He recalled that Lyon later had the dubious honor of being the first Union general to die in battle.

Throughout the war years Shad had managed to settle in comfortably with the Pomeroy family. He went to school, getting a better education than he could have dreamed of. During those years, he grew to manhood. By the time he was old enough to enlist in the Union Army, the surrender at Appomattox ended the fighting.

Shad was reading for the law at the Pomeroy & Gates Law Firm when he decided to return home. He said good-bye to the family that had sheltered him and headed for Colorado Territory.

It hadn't taken him long to relearn the skills that he'd abandoned years before. For a time, he worked in the Trinidad area where he'd spent his boyhood. He took a liking to the outdoors and to ranching. Then, wanting to put some distance between himself and the Judge's watchful eye, he'd ridden north and hired on with Crane's outfit.

Of his own blood kin, he had none. At least none that he knew of. His mother had died before he was old enough to remember her. There was only his father's loving description to link him with the woman who'd once been the most important person in his life.

Throughout the time since Dunham Wakefield's death, Shad had often felt alone. Friends like Judge Madison, Abe, and Charlie had eased that feeling from time to time, but it always returned. Somewhere along the way, he'd made a kind of truce with loneliness, and he'd learned to live with it. Now, it was a strength, for in truth he needed only himself.

Back in St. Louis, there had been a girl that he wanted to marry. Letitia was a friend of Sophie Pomeroy, the Judge's niece. From the first, he'd been taken by her lively, fun-loving way, not to mention the fact that she was beautiful. She had creamy skin, and mahogany-colored hair, and large dark eyes that a fellow could fall into and drown. She'd discreetly flirted with him, and he'd returned her interest. They had spent time together at parties, and she often came to visit Sophie, giving them a chance to get to know each other. He couldn't say just when he began to think of marrying her and living the prosperous life of a city lawyer. But suddenly, without warning, her family moved back to Ohio, taking Letitia with them. He'd been devastated and was making plans to follow, when Sophie got word that Letitia was engaged to an Ohio congressman. It was soon after that Shad made his decision to leave St. Louis. In his pain, he felt the need to return to the kind of life that he'd led as a boy.

Abe roused him from his melancholy thoughts. "It looks like we're dealing with one nasty outlaw, that's clear," he said.

"I'd sure like to have a look at Rumbaugh's place," Shad said. "I wonder if it's as impregnable as they say it is."

"I expect it's well fortified," said Abe, "even though he's going to have to draw off some of his men to secure the Craddock ranch. A man in Rumbaugh's position has to be prepared. I doubt if we could even get close without some of his men picking us off."

Shad figured that Rumbaugh's one weakness was the fact that he'd have to divide his forces from now on.

Everyone within miles around knew that Craddock had relatives, and the ranch should rightfully go to them. He tried to remember what he'd heard about them, and recalled that there was a nephew living in Denver City. There was a niece someplace too. If they showed up and challenged Rumbaugh's claim, he'd have to defend it with men and guns, for he couldn't do it in a courtroom. Craddock had filed on that land and had built the house himself. There was one other ominous possibility. The land-grabbing rancher could kill the heirs.

Rumbaugh was having everything his own way, and Shad decided it was time to put the outlaw on notice. Nobody should be allowed to get away with murder, or robbery, or ordering a man to be lynched. It was time for Charlie's killer to start worrying.

They rode back toward Kaminski's ranch, all the while keeping a sharp look-out for unfriendly riders. At one point, they sought the cover of a draw and rode for a long distance within its sheltering sides. When they started out of it, Shad caught sight of riders in the distance.

"Get down!" he ordered.

They waited in the draw for a long time, giving the riders a chance move on.

"Those had to be Rumbaugh's men," Shad said. "I know all the Circle C hands real well, and none of them were riding with that bunch."

It was a good bet that they were out looking for him, and he hoped that Kaminski didn't run into trouble. He especially hoped that Mc Nary didn't run into them, for Rumbaugh's men knew him well, and most likely they'd shoot him on sight.

Night caught up with them and they made another cold camp. Shad was getting used to roughing it, although he didn't like it much. He was too fond of warm food and hot coffee. But he was thankful that it wasn't winter, or they'd have to dig themselves out of the snow come morning.

Abe took the first watch, while Shad crawled into his blankets and dropped off to sleep. He hadn't gotten

much rest, though, before Abe was shaking him
awake.

"Quick, look over there," he said, pointing.

In the distance, a big red and orange glow lighted
up the dark sky.

Shad crawled out of his bedroll, rubbed sleep from
his eyes, and took a second look.

"Isn't that about where Kaminski's house and barn
are located?" Abe asked. "Those were Rumbaugh's
men we saw earlier. They must have set the fire."

Shad got a sick feeling in his gut. He figured that
Abe was right. It was Kaminski's place that was on
fire, and Rumbaugh's men most likely had set it. His
next reaction was anger. His enemies had tracked him
to Kaminski's, and not finding him there, they'd gone
and torched the place out of spite.

"I sure hope them two cowhands got out of there
okay," Abe said. "And I hope that Kaminski and Mc
Nary wasn't back yet with any of the others."

Shad seconded that. All the while, he couldn't take
his eyes off the light, knowing that a good man's
dream and hard work was going up in flames.

When it got daylight, they rode out.

When they got closer to the smoking ruins, they
entered the draw where they'd planned to meet the
others. They made their way along it until they
reached the place where they could see a couple of
Rumbaugh's men lounging nearby with rifles in their
hands. The outlaws looked bored and tired.

Then something else caught Shad's attention. There
were two freshly dug graves not far from the remains

of the barn. If anyone doubted that Rumbaugh meant business, those graves were their proof. It didn't take much to figure out that Kaminski's men, Scruggs and Henley, were dead.

He silently pointed them out to Abe, who shook his head sadly.

"Rumbaugh left two men to guard the place," he whispered. "It looks to me like he's spreading his manpower awful thin. If it wasn't for all the help your boss is givin' him, he'd be in a bind for sure."

It came back to Luke Crane again. Shad vowed that if he lived through this, he'd settle the score with Crane, and he figured the most satisfactory way to do it was with his fists.

They waited in the draw some distance away until Rumbaugh's men turned their attention to breakfast. It was then that Shad gave the signal to attack. Together, he and Abe rode out of their hiding place and bore down on the outlaws.

They heard them coming.

"It's Wakefield," one of them yelled as he grabbed for his gun, unmindful that his food and coffee got spilled in the process.

The other one went for his gun, too, but they were both too slow.

"Hold it!" Shad ordered. "We've got you dead to rights."

Both men put their hands in the air. They had no choice but to surrender, for they were looking down the barrels of two Colts.

"What are you going to do with us?" asked one in a squeaky voice that Shad recognized from the night he lay wounded on the mountain.

"I'm going to tie you up and then I'm going to turn you over to the law," he replied.

The other one laughed.

"What law? You don't really think you can get away with this, do you? All of the boss's men are combing this part of the Territory for you, and all of Crane's men are, too, since they think you killed one of your own."

It was hard to do, but Shad fought down the urge to hit Squeaky Voice in the mouth.

"You and the rest of Rumbaugh's outfit are going to pay for that killing, and for all the other killings that you've done, before this is over," he promised.

"Especially those two poor hapless fellows that you killed last night," Abe added, nodding toward the graves.

"It was their own tough luck," said Squeaky Voice. "They was dumb enough to be workin' for the wrong side."

While Shad kept them covered, Abe brought over enough rope to tie them up. Then he proceeded to do so in spite of their loud complaints.

"Might as well finish up the breakfast that they left," he said when he was finished. "At least the part of it they didn't spill on the ground."

Abe seemed to enjoy badgering the two outlaws so Shad went along.

"Yep, it'd be a sin to let it all go to waste," he agreed.

Rumbaugh's men looked on with grim expressions as he and Abe finished their meal. Nearby was the still-smoking ruins of Kaminski's house and barn.

"Outlawin' ain't all a man expects it to be, is it?" Abe needled them.

"The boss's going to get you both for this," said Squeaky's partner. "You're out of your minds for being here."

"Guess a man's got a right to express his opinion," Abe responded mildly.

Shad suspected that the two of them had been on burial detail, and they were either to wait for the rest of the gang to return, or they were to join them after their chore was done. In either case, Rumbaugh would soon know that something had gone wrong. This meant that they couldn't stay, and if Mc Nary, Kaminski, or the Osborns happened to come back at the wrong time, they could run into big trouble.

"We'd better get a move on," he said. "We've got work to do."

"Who are we going to warn first?" Abe asked, realizing the danger. "The Osborns?"

"Yeah. We'd better start with them and add them to our number. If we should run into that gang it might make a big difference."

With the two outlaws to guard, he and Abe couldn't very well split up, with one of them going to warn Kaminski or Mc Nary. Instead, they were going to have to do it the slow way, sticking together. But just as they were starting off with the outlaws in tow, he spotted two riders coming toward them.

"Hold it a minute, Abe," he said. "That looks like Kaminski with that fellow he was going to bring back with him."

Abe shielded his eyes and peered into the distance. "I believe you're right."

When they rode up, Kaminski stayed in the saddle and surveyed the ruins of his ranch. He had a look of shock on his face. The others permitted him a solemn moment to try and absorb what had happened.

"We're sure sorry about your loss," Abe said, speaking for both of them. "A man puts his own sweat and blood into building a place like this, and it's hard to look on such vicious destruction and killing."

Kaminski pointed at the graves.

"My men Scruggs and Henley?" he asked.

Abe nodded. "I expect so," he said. There was another respectful silence while Kaminski absorbed the terrible truth.

"You were right about Rumbaugh, my friend," said the man called Loftis. "That man is dang sure of himself. He's flaunting his power and he's got no conscience."

Loftis was tall and rail thin, with a long face that held deeply grooved lines. To Shad, he looked more like a parson or an undertaker than someone who could lead the tough life of a rancher. But in his favor, he was willing to fight for the kind of land that Colorado Territory was meant to be. That went a long way in Shad's book.

"Wakefield, was it them two men that did the killing?" Kaminski asked, pointing to the prisoners.

"They were in on it. They were left behind to do the burying."

"What are you going to do with them?"

"Turn them over to the law, whenever and wherever we can find some."

"With Rumbaugh and his outfit on the loose, we might not get the chance."

"Oh, you can count on that," said Squeaky.

They ignored him.

"We'll just bring 'em along with us," said Shad. "That'll make two less guns for Rumbaugh."

"Shad, we'd better get a move on and go find the Osborns," Abe reminded him. "It wouldn't do for them to ride in here, and maybe get themselves killed if the outlaws decide to come back for their partners."

"And what about your friend, Mc Nary?" Kaminski asked.

"We're mighty concerned about him and the Beales," Abe replied. "From the direction of their tracks, Rumbaugh and his bunch might have been headed that way. If we can pick up the Osborns, then together we might all stand a chance."

"This is turning out to be a war," Loftis observed. "What else could you call it?"

As far as Shad was concerned, Loftis was right. This was a war to determine how people were going to live in a Territory of the United States, as well as who would be dispossessed and who would die. What's more, their side needed all the men it could get.

"Let's ride," he said.

They were headed for the Osborn ranch when they spotted the two brothers riding toward them. A dust cloud billowed up in their wake. When they reached Shad and the others, they reined up.

"What a pity," Cletus said pointing toward the smoking ruins. "What happened?"

"I got burned out," said Kaminski. "Rumbaugh's bunch did it."

"We were coming to warn you away," Shad explained. "These two sidewinders that we've got the ropes on are part of the gang, and the rest will likely come back when they don't show up. They stayed behind to bury Kaminski's two men that they killed."

"It's a sad day," Cletus said, shaking his head, "a sad day, indeed."

"Well, we're pleased to have you join us," said Shad. "We've got to get to the Beale's ranch *pronto*. Mc Nary went to recruit them, and it looks like the outlaws may have gone that way, too."

He noticed that Squeaky started looking uneasy as he listened to their plans. His surly-faced friend didn't seem any too happy, either.

"There's six of us, now," Abe said. "Let's go and find out what's keeping Mc Nary. I sure wouldn't want nothing bad to happen to that boy, seein' as how I was the one that invited him along in the first place."

The morning had slipped by, and time was growing short. With the prisoners in tow, they headed in the direction of the Diamond B, the name of the Beale ranch. It was the spread that was the farthest away. The sun had slipped below the horizon awhile before they got there, and they rode the remaining distance in darkness with only the stars and the light from a quarter moon to see by. Finally Shad spotted the shadowy outline of Joe Beale's house. He and the others reined up.

"Well," Kaminski said, "if Rumbaugh and the no-accounts that work for him were here, at least they didn't burn the place down."

"Still, we'd better be careful," Abe warned. "That outfit could be holed up down there just waiting for us to come riding in. It sure wouldn't be much trouble for them to pick us off one by one."

Shad voiced his doubts. "The place has a deserted look about it. If they've been here, I think they've gone, but I agree that we need to be cautious. Why don't I ride in there alone while the rest of you wait here and keep me covered?"

"Make it the two of us," Abe said, "and I'll agree."

Shad didn't want to argue about it, and he was learning from experience that Abe usually got his own way.

"Come on, then," he conceded. "Kaminski, if either of the prisoners so much as lets out a whimper, put 'em to sleep with the butt of your gun."

"It'd be my pleasure, Wakefield," said the big

rancher with enthusiasm. "These two no-accounts won't be warning anybody."

Shad and Abe made their way forward on foot, moving as quietly as two shadows. They circled around and approached the ranch on its blind side. But just as they were closing in on the adobe structure, a voice commanded them to halt and drop their guns. The voice sounded familiar.

"Mc Nary, is that you?" Shad called.

A dark figure stepped around the corner of the house. "Glad to see you, Wakefield," he said. "I thought it was some of Rumbaugh's outfit coming back to take another look around the place."

It appeared that Shad's hunch had been right.

"Then the outlaws have been here," he said. "We were afraid of that. What's happened to the Beales?"

"Cory, you and Joe can come on out," Mc Nary called. "You, too, Trujillo. This time it's the good guys who've come to visit."

The Beales and one of their cowhands emerged from behind a lean-to.

"We saw the outlaws coming and we slipped out the back way," Mc Nary said. "There was too many of 'em for us to hole up in here and fight it out, so we slipped away and hid ourselves in the tall grass. They didn't find us, but they stole our horses and whatever else they could lay their hands on."

Grama grass and other weeds grew tall enough to hide a man who was hunkered down. Shad was relieved that Mc Nary, Trujillo, and the Beales had been smart enough to hide rather than force a confrontation. They'd also been lucky that Rumbaugh's men were more interested in pilfering than in going out and beating the bushes to find them.

Shad whistled for Kaminski and the others to ride on in.

"Why do you think Rumbaugh is raiding the surrounding ranches all of a sudden?" Cory Beale asked.

Shad had met Cory, who was a few years younger than himself, when he first came up from Trinidad. He came across as being more of a kid than a grown man.

"I expect Rumbaugh has had it on his mind for a long time," Abe replied. "It's just that he'd planned to encroach little by little, one place at a time, so's he wouldn't get everyone stirred up until it was too late to do anything. When Shad and his pardner caught 'em murderin' Ben Craddock, and when Shad got away from 'em, he figured the jig was up. Being sneaky about it just ain't possible any more, so it looks like he's goin' ahead full steam."

"Yeah," said Kaminski, "Luke Crane is the only one around here who hasn't seen him for what he is."

"Crane had better watch out," Mc Nary warned. "Rumbaugh doesn't suffer fools for long, only until he doesn't have any more use for 'em."

Shad figured that whatever Rumbaugh dished out to Crane was exactly what he had coming to him. When he struggled to be more charitable in his thinking, he failed. Crane didn't merit any charity.

"Are we going to attack them?" asked Loftis, his voice betraying his nervousness. "And if so, when?"

It was a good question, and Shad was able to see clearly in the moonlight that they had all turned to him for the answer.

Chapter Four

Rumbaugh's forces outnumbered the ten of them. A direct attack on the fortified Lazy R would mean disaster. Shad had to find another way. There wasn't any doubt that the Craddock ranch was guarded too. Still, it would be by far the more vulnerable of the two places. He let his mind wander over the possibilities. A surprise attack was the only way, and that would mean an attack in the darkness. If they were able to capture the outlaws who were posted at the Craddock ranch, it would cut Rumbaugh's forces severely, and put him on the defensive for the first time. But holding the place would be another matter. Rumbaugh would undoubtedly lay siege. They'd be trapped like helpless animals and starved out. The best way, he decided, was to attack and do as much damage as possible, then withdraw. This would leave Rumbaugh worrying about when and where they'd strike next.

The others awaited his orders.

"Rumbaugh's place is out, at least for now," he said. "Our first attack will be at the Box C. If we can take them by surprise, we might have a chance."

"Sounds like the smart way," Abe agreed.

"But first we've got to learn what we can," Shad went on. "We have to know how many of his men he's got there and where they're positioned. But even before that, we need to find a place where we can hole up and stay out of sight. I guess I don't need to mention that we don't want Crane, or any of his outfit, to spot us, either."

"What about the old Purdy shack?" Mc Nary suggested. "We could be there before daylight, and nobody's apt to spot us riding at night."

Shad approved of the idea. The Purdy shack was about as close to the Craddock place as they dared to get with any hope of not being seen. Him and Charlie had sheltered there the night before Charlie was killed. There had been signs that others had done the same thing from time to time. The shack was surrounded by some old cottonwoods, several large overgrown lilacs, and great bunches of other shrubs that thrived on the abandoned home site. The trees and shrubs would serve to provide a screen for them and their horses.

"That's a good idea, Mc Nary," Shad agreed. "We'll use the old Purdy shack for a hideout."

"Don't forget that Mc Nary, Trujillo, and the Beales need mounts," Abe reminded him.

This was true, for the four of them would be riding the spare horses, the ones which needed to be held in reserve.

"I'll go back to my place and fetch some horses and provisions over to the Purdy shack," Slim Osborn volunteered.

"Another good idea," said Shad. "Just be careful. Try not to let anyone see where you're taking them."

"I'll do my best. If I'm spotted, I'll simply head off in a different direction and go a roundabout way."

"Then good luck to you."

Slim Osborn rode off, disappearing into the night like a wraith.

"What about sending word for the U.S. Marshal?" Abe said. "Looks to me like it's about time to get one down here."

"I'm not against it," Shad replied. "But that's going to take time, and time is something we don't have. We've got to act now before the outlaws burn any more of the ranches, or kill any more people. Besides, Judge Madison knows what's going on, at least part of it. I expect he'll notify the authorities, and they'll send a marshal down one of these days when they get around to it."

"You've got a point there, son, and I agree that if something's going to be done, we're the ones who're going to have to do it."

The group of allies headed toward their chosen hideout, along with the prisoners. Shad had spent many nights under the Colorado sky, and he'd done a lot of night riding. He'd come to appreciate it as a good time

for thinking. As he rode beside the others, he wondered what his life would have been like if he'd mar-
ried Letitia, as he had wanted so badly to do. Most
certainly he'd have remained in St. Louis practicing
law. The words that came to his mind now to describe
that kind of life were *staid* and *predictable*. He knew,
now, that he simply wasn't cut out for practicing law
in St. Louis or any other big city. Fate had been kind
to him when it had taken Letitia away to marry the
Ohio legislator, although he'd been too miserable at
the time to understand this. The sort of woman he
needed was a far cry from the delicate, fragile house-
plant that Letitia had been. What he needed was a
wildflower that could survive in adverse conditions,
and still manage to thrive and be lovely. But a wildflower woman was rare.

They arrived at the shack before sunrise and teth-
ered the horses in the midst of the shrubs. Shad had
heard the story of the Purdys. A man, his wife, and
his brother-in-law had come from Indiana and settled
here. Together they'd built the place. But after a time,
the woman had taken ill. Then both her brother and
her husband came down with the same malady. All
three had died, leaving their small home to deteriorate.
There was a stream not far from the house, and while
there were times when it ran dry, this wasn't one of
them. There would be water enough for all of them,
and for their animals as well.

It was shortly after sunrise when Abe took it upon
himself to cook breakfast. He built a campfire beneath
the trees so that the smoke would be filtered to invi-

sibility by the leaves. He soon managed to produce a quantity of crisp bacon and light johnnycake, enough for everyone to eat hearty. After they finished the meal and were sitting around, Shad noticed that young Cory Beale was pacing like a caged animal. Whatever it was that surges through a man and makes him ready for battle was surging through the youngest member of their outfit. Usually this readiness was an asset, but sometimes it could be a liability, causing a man to do something foolish. He needed to find a task that would keep Cory busy and out of trouble. It turned out that he wasn't the only one who was thinking along those lines.

"Maybe we ought to have someone ride over toward the Osborn ranch," Abe suggested. "Might be they'd run into Slim and maybe give him a hand. I expect he could use some help, and I was thinkin' that Cory, here, would be a good man to send."

Before Shad could open his mouth to agree, Cory was already protesting.

"Nothin' doing. The chances are good that I wouldn't run into him, and he don't need my help anyway. Look, I've got an idea about something that would make a big difference. Is anybody interested in hearing what it is?"

"I'm interested," Abe said. "I reckon we all are."

Shad and the others agreed.

Now that everyone's attention was on him, Cory Beale looked self-conscious.

"I was just thinking," he said, "that we need to put a man inside the Rumbaugh camp to find out what it is they're up to. I can be that man since they don't know me very well. I can tell them that Uncle Joe and me had a big falling out, and that I'm striking out on my own and need a job."

"Nothing doing," his uncle protested. "Boy, you ain't got no idea what you'd be gettin' yourself into."

Shad could see Cory's color rise at being called a boy in front of the men whom he considered to be his peers. To make matters worse, Mc Nary spoke up with an opinion contrary to what Cory wanted to hear.

"Look, Beale, I've worked for Rumbaugh, and I learned the hard way that he's mean and he's unpredictable. You'd better not risk riding into his stronghold all by yourself. If he was to catch you trying to put one over on him, he'd kill you on the spot."

Cory glared at him, but he backed down.

"Okay, if that's the way you feel about it, forget what I said. But I'm not going off on some fool's errand, either."

Shad would have preferred to have him safely out of the way. But at least he'd been talked out of doing something dangerous and stupid.

"No fool's errands," Abe agreed.

Shad hoped that Cory would settle down and stop causing problems. But the kid's pent-up energy was obvious. That, along with the belligerent expression on his face, warned Shad not to count on a lot of cooperation.

It had been a long night, and they were all short on sleep and tired to the bone. After drawing straws for guard duty, they all turned in, leaving Loftis to keep watch. Shad figured that Slim Osborn would show up sometime in the afternoon—that is, if he didn't run into some kind of trouble. He was glad to see that Slim's brother, Cletus, had been holding up well, in spite of his injured leg. The Osborns were men you could depend on.

Shad had no idea how much time had passed before something woke him. He wasn't even sure what had done it, but he had a gut feeling that something was wrong. All around him were the sounds of sleeping men. He opened his eyes to slits just wide enough to see through, and with a minimum of movement, he surveyed the campsite. The prisoners were still bound and appeared to be dozing. Everyone else was asleep, too, even Loftis, who was supposed to be standing guard. Shad got up, keeping his hand close to his revolver. He walked over to where Loftis was sprawled on the ground. The guard's rifle lay nearby, as if he'd dropped it when he fell. It was plain that Loftis hadn't gone to sleep on his own. He'd had considerable help. There was a big purple bruise on the side of his head where he'd been slugged. A quick glance around the camp told Shad what he already suspected. The only one missing was Cory Beale, and he'd taken one of the horses. Shad figured Beale could thank his good luck that he hadn't taken off with the sorrel or the line-back dun. Shad would have considered that a theft of the most serious kind and would have had Beale's hide for it. It was bad enough that the fellow had injured a man who trusted him and considered him a friend. All this was done so he could ride off on a hair-brained scheme that was sure to get him killed, and just might get the rest of them killed as well.

He rolled Loftis over on his back and tried to revive him. Abe woke up then, and came over to help.

"So Cory went and flew the coop, did he? I was afraid something like this might happen, but I'd hoped he'd have the maturity and good sense to follow orders and stay here with the rest of us."

"Guess we both expected too much, Abe."

"What the blazes is going on?" Joe Beale demanded to know as the rest of the outfit started waking up.

"Your nephew knocked Loftis in the head and took off on one of the horses," Shad informed him. "How about going over and soaking this bandana in the spring? Maybe some cold water on his face will help to bring him around."

Joe Beale swore under his breath, took the bandana, and headed for the spring.

Kaminski came over and looked down at the unconscious man.

"You really don't think that young whelp is going over to Rumbaugh's place to get hired on, do you?"

"I expect you'd be safe to bet your last dollar on it," Shad replied. "And if they're suspicious, it won't take them any time at all to knock the truth out of him about where it is that we're hid out, and what we're planning to do."

Kaminski scowled. "I surely wish I had my hands on that young fool right now," he said.

Joe Beale returned, carrying the wet cloth for Loftis's head. He overheard Shad's grim prognosis and Kaminski's angry response.

"They're apt to kill that boy, aren't they?"

Nobody answered, but their silence must have been a confirmation of his fear.

"Well, he ain't a bad kid," Joe defended his nephew. "He's just bullheaded and hot-tempered. He hasn't got a lick of common sense. My brother never did either, so he come by it honest. But whatever he did, he don't deserve to die. Can't we do something?"

Try as he might, Shad couldn't come up with anything that didn't entail an action that would be suicidal. Neither could any of the others.

"This is one time the boy is going to have to fend for himself," Abe said quietly. "But he's determined and he's smart, so maybe he'll be able to pull it off."

"But just in case he doesn't, we'd better haul ourselves out of here," Kaminski said. "If they're suspicious and they make him talk, they'll be coming after us."

Even though Shad knew this was true, he regretted having to leave. The shack was a perfect hideout. He didn't want Cory Beale to lose his life, either, but the way he was feeling at the moment, he wouldn't mind too much if the outlaws roughed him up a little.

Loftis moaned, a sign that he was coming around. Shad was glad to hear it, but he knew the injured man was destined to have the granddaddy of all headaches.

"What happened?" Loftis asked as he struggled to sit up.

Abe explained about Cory Beale's defection.

"Why, that kid is so dumb he couldn't drive a nail into a snowbank," Loftis exclaimed, "but I guess I'm even dumber for trusting him."

"No, that black mark has to go on my account," said Shad. "After the way he was talking earlier, somebody should have been assigned to keep an eye on him. I underestimated how far he'd go, and now we're all having to pay for my mistake."

Abe helped Loftis to his feet, where he took a few unsteady steps.

"Can you ride?" Abe asked him.

"I don't know, but I'm sure going to try."

Shad had his doubts, but he knew they dared not stay at the shack. He was concerned about Slim Osborn, too. He should be there with the horses. As it was, he'd have no way of knowing about this new trouble they were in, and he wouldn't know where to follow with the needed mounts and supplies. There was also the danger that he'd run into the outlaws who were still out searching. Shad decided to risk waiting another hour.

Pretty soon, Kaminski spotted Osborn riding toward the shack with a half dozen horses tied on lead ropes.

"Here he comes, just like he said he would."

By the time Osborn rode into camp, they were all loaded up.

"Hey, what's the hurry?" he asked.

"We've got trouble," Abe told him.

"More than usual?"

"Yeah. More than usual."

Quickly, Abe filled him in on what had happened.

Slim looked like he couldn't believe anyone would pull such a dumb stunt as Cory had. But probably out of respect for Joe, he held his tongue.

Together, Shad and Abe hoisted the injured Loftis into the saddle. He looked pale and drawn, but he never uttered a sound of complaint.

"Where are we off to?" Kaminski asked when everyone was mounted and ready to go.

"It appears to me that we don't have a lot of choices," said Shad. "But there's a little valley over closer to the Craddock place. It's hardly big enough to call a valley, but we'd be surrounded by small hills that would give us some cover."

"Is that where you and your pardner saw the shooting?" Abe asked.

"Yeah. You can see the whole place from the top of one of the hills."

"I know where it is you're talking about," Joe said. "It's located awful close to the enemy, though."

"It just means that we won't have to ride so far when we attack. It also means that we can keep an eye on the place."

"Then if everybody agrees, we'd better hie ourselves out of here *pronto*," said Abe.

Nine men and their two prisoners rode away from the decaying shack, leaving it abandoned one more time.

Chapter Five

Jake Rumbaugh leaned back in his big hide-covered chair and lit one of the cigars that had come all the way from Trinidad. It was an indulgence that he felt he deserved. After all, he'd just returned from a strenuous ride that had lasted for days, instead of the few hours that he'd expected. But then nothing had gone the way he'd planned, beginning with those two saddle bums making an appearance just when he was disposing of Craddock. That was something he couldn't have foreseen, and it had caused him to waste precious time in a pursuit that had ended in failure. It had also forced him to show his hand. He realized that he was on dangerous ground now, but he was convinced that if he acted swiftly, his plan was salvageable. It was a satisfaction that Luke Crane, at least, had fallen into line. His spiel, which was backed up by his men, had persuaded Crane that Wakefield was a killer. If only the man had been smart enough to find Wakefield and hang him before the saddle bum could cause even more trouble than he had already. But Crane and all of his men had failed too. No question about it, Wakefield lived a charmed life.

If the killing hadn't been witnessed, he could have taken charge of the Craddock Ranch with nobody being the wiser about how he got it. He could simply have said that Craddock had sold him the place before leaving the country. A forged signature, one of his many skills, would have eased suspicions if anyone challenged him. But the way it was now, things had gotten complicated. There were too many in the area who wouldn't believe that Wakefield had killed his partner and the old rancher. It was unfortunate that not everybody was as gullible and hot-headed as Luke Crane. If only they were, it would make his task a lot easier.

He took a satisfying puff on his cigar, enjoying the aroma. With a glance, he surveyed the room that was his pride and pleasure. It smelled of the beeswax that Talasi, his Indian housekeeper, used to polish the furniture. It also smelled of leather bindings and good cigars. This was his office, and it was as much like his father's, back in Philadelphia, as he could make it. The mahogany desk that he'd imported from St. Louis, at great expense, was its centerpiece. A beautifully crafted bookshelf stood against one of the walls. It contained no less than thirty-seven books. That was one volume for each year of his life, and he'd read them all. He wasn't stupid, which was what his father had accused him of being that day he'd walked off, leaving his son to the not-so-gentle handling of the jailors. The look of disgust on Carlton Rumbaugh's face, just before he'd turned away, no longer haunted him. He told himself that it never had. After all, Carlton Rumbaugh was never anything but a small-time businessman. He, on the other hand, was holding a couple of large ranches, and he would soon take over half a dozen more. Combined, all of those ranches would make up a sizeable piece of Colorado. They represented wealth and they represented power. With wealth and power at hand, it didn't matter about past humiliations, or the fact that he was too short and was getting a paunch, or that the pretty women wouldn't give him the time of day.

But he was going to have to be very careful from now on, for there simply wasn't room for any more blunders.

Suddenly, his peace was disturbed by a commotion outside. Someone was yelling. He struggled out of the chair and went over to the window that had been recently fitted with glass panes. It appeared that some of his men had a stranger surrounded. One of them turned and headed toward the house at a trot. Rumbaugh went to the door to let him in.

"What's going on out there?" he demanded to know.

"Boss, there's a fellow outside who claims that he wants to hire on."

"Well, we need all the hands we can get. What's the trouble about hiring him?"

"He's Cory Beale, Joe Beale's nephew."

Rumbaugh took a step back in surprise. *What was young Beale doing here?* He also wondered if the kid's uncle knew about his nephew's defection. But then again, maybe it was his uncle who'd sent him, thinking that a relative in Rumbaugh's employ would make him immune to further raids. *Maybe he's been sent here to spy.*

"Well, Boss, what should we do about the kid?"

Beale was an unknown and unexpected factor, and Rumbaugh didn't like the unknown or the unexpected. *Best to keep him around and keep an eye on him.*

"Hire him," he said. "I'll have a talk with him later on."

The man whose name he couldn't quite remember looked surprised at his orders. But he, like the others, had learned not to question them. While Rumbaugh watched, his hired hand turned and hurried back to the others.

Rumbaugh ate a hearty supper that had been cooked by the lovely Talasi before summoning Beale to his office. One look told him that the kid was wet behind the ears and plenty scared to boot. He imagined that it didn't help Beale's peace of mind that he'd been disarmed before being allowed to enter the house.

"Sit down," Rumbaugh ordered.

The kid sat, almost missing the chair in his nervousness.

"How come you to leave your own ranch and come riding way over here looking for work?" Rumbaugh asked.

He watched Beale's Adam's apple bob up and down as he swallowed hard before answering.

"It's not my ranch. That's the trouble. It's my uncle's place and he never listens to me. He does things the way he wants to, not the way I think they should be done. I got sick and tired of him telling me that he's the boss, so I figured it was time for me to go off on my own. They say that you pay your hands top wages."

Rumbaugh liked his answer. He'd felt the same way about his own father, who'd believed it was his duty and privilege to order his son around. He'd also been quick with his tongue lashings, usually in front of others, no matter how well his son had performed. Rumbaugh could picture himself, back then, doing the same thing that Beale was doing now. Still, he didn't trust the kid. In all fairness, however, he trusted no one.

"If you don't like following orders," he said, "maybe you'd better climb back onto that horse of yours and head out of here right now, because you're certainly going to follow mine or regret the first one that you don't."

He watched Beale turn a couple of shades paler.

"Following orders would be different if they came from you," he stammered.

Rumbaugh leaned forward, placing his hands on the desk and looking the kid straight in the eye. "And how is that?" he asked.

"Because I'd be getting paid real good to follow them, and that's a big change."

Rumbaugh kept looking at him a moment longer, enjoying Beale's extreme discomfiture.

"You'd better be telling me the truth," he said at last, "because if you're not, the chances are you're going to end up dead."

"I've got no reason to lie," Beale protested. "It's just like I said. I want to make my own way and not have to answer to my uncle."

"Then get out of here. My men crawl out of bed early and they earn their pay."

It amused him to watch the kid almost tip the chair over in his haste to leave. Young Beale had a lot to learn, especially about hiding his fear.

As soon as Talasi had escorted his new hired hand out the front door, Rumbaugh signaled his foreman, Red Courtney, to come in from the back room. Courtney was a burly man with hair the color of his nickname.

"You think he's on the up and up?" Courtney asked.

"Maybe. Maybe not. You'd better keep an eye on him. If we have to, we can always get rid of him later."

"That uncle of his has friends."

"Him and his uncle are on the outs. Didn't you hear?"

"I heard. It don't mean that I believe it."

"Well, we'll just have to see. I need more men, and it might be that he's what he says he is, a young fellow who wants to strike out on his own."

"Then I'll be keeping a sharp look-out where he's concerned, and I'll pass the word along for the others to do the same. If that Beale kid so much as breathes wrong, I intend to know about it."

"That's the kind of thing that I'm paying you for," Rumbaugh reminded him.

When his foreman had gone, he reached for the humidor to get another cigar. He'd tried to limit himself so that he wouldn't run out before he could resupply at Trinidad. But the past few days had been tough ones, and a good cigar was soothing to his nerves. It also helped him to think, and this was something he needed to do.

He worried about Craddock's heirs showing up and claiming their inheritance. He had the forged bill of sale to fall back on, but he was loathe to use it. It would be especially shaky if rumors of the murder got around. On the other hand, he had possession of the ranch, and it would take a lot of force to compel him to give it up. Not to mention that Kaminski was apt to be pulling out since his place had burned. Watching it go up in flames had given Rumbaugh a lot of satisfaction. That Polish immigrant had been troublesome for a long time.

There was no getting around his most urgent problem, though. He needed more men. But if he couldn't recruit additional gun hands, he'd make do somehow. Working in his favor was the fact that the two-bit ranchers in the area weren't organized, and the largest rancher was a thick-headed man who couldn't find his own backside in the daylight. Thanks mostly to him, Wakefield was running for his life.

Thinking about this made Rumbaugh feel a whole lot better. It helped to ease the aggravation of all the setbacks he'd endured. He was on the offensive and he was determined to stay on the offensive. One day soon, he'd have it all—all he'd ever dreamed of—or else he'd know the reason why.

He was rudely yanked from his thoughts by the sound of someone pounding on the front door.

"What in blazes!"

He looked around for Talasi, but she'd evidently gone to bed. He got up and went to open the door himself. When he did, he found Red Courtney standing there in the stream of lamplight that spilled from the doorway. There was another fellow beside him.

"Koch, here, rode in from the Craddock place with urgent news," Courtney said.

"Well? Let's hear it."

"Something's happened that you ought to know about," Koch started to explain.

"Then stop beating around the bush and out with it."

"It's Craddock's kin. They rode in today from Denver City. The nephew says him and his sister are taking charge of their inheritance, meaning the whole bloomin' ranch."

So, somebody had gotten word to them; he'd been afraid of that. He'd hoped to avoid trouble in that direction, but it wasn't to be.

"What did you do with them?"

"Well, they acted real uppity like they was the owners, so we let 'em. Figured you could handle it whatever way you saw fit."

"Yes. You did right. I wonder if anyone else around here knows they've arrived."

"They didn't mention it. Maybe."

That "maybe" was what was causing the problem for Rumbaugh. If no one else knew about their arrival, he could just dispose of them and go on about his business. But if anyone had seen them, he'd have to come up with a way to explain their disappearance.

"Was it just the two of them?" he asked.

"Yeah."

"Okay, go saddle my horse. Courtney, you and a couple of others get ready to ride. Bring along that Beale kid, too."

"I'll get right to it," Courtney said before the two men disappeared into the night.

Rumbaugh closed the door and went back to his office where he buckled on his gunbelt. Next, he shrugged into his jacket. He assured himself that this wasn't anything to be overly concerned about. He just had a couple of loose ends to take care of, and this was a skill that he was getting to be very good at.

By the time Courtney returned with his horse, Rumbaugh had convinced himself that he'd actually enjoy taking a nice moonlight ride.

He mounted up and rode out with Courtney, Beale, and two others, whose names he couldn't quite remember.

Chapter Six

Shad had noticed that the men were edgy, which was to be expected since they were camped so close to an enemy stronghold. He didn't feel any too comfortable about it himself. Their camp wouldn't be an easy position to defend should they be discovered, but it was the only place he could think of that would serve their needs. He regretted that they had to abandon the shack, and wished he'd prevented the foolish action that had caused its loss.

"I sure hope they don't send out patrols," Kaminski said, "but they might do it, just as a matter of routine. We'd better keep alert."

Shad had been concerned about patrols, too, not that the lot of them couldn't handle a couple of outlaws. But gunshots would bring the others down on them like hornets prodded from their nest. Not to mention that if Cory's plan failed, Rumbaugh and his gun hands would go to the Purdy shack and track them from there. Since surprise was their sole advantage, Shad couldn't afford to lose it.

In the moonlight, he saw that Loftis was sitting off to the side, away from the others. He was resting his head in his hands. Shad walked over to him.

"Are you okay?" he inquired.

Loftis looked up at him, moving his head as little as possible in the process.

"Well, if you don't count a pain in my noggin as big as Texas, you could say that I'm just fine."

"You might have to fight no matter how bad you feel."

"Oh, I'll do my part. Don't you worry none about that."

Shad believed him, and since there was nothing he could do to help, he walked away, leaving him to nurse his aching head. He went over to his saddlebags and fished out a pair of field glasses.

"What is it you're up to?" asked Abe, who'd been watching.

"I'm going to climb up there and see if I can make out the number of men that have been posted over at Craddock's." He pointed toward the top of the rise that overlooked the distant ranch house.

"I expect they'd all be in the bunkhouse by now, except for a few of them that's been put on guard duty."

"I know. But at least I can get some kind of idea about how things are."

S.J. Stewart

"Suit yourself. It sure can't hurt nothin'. You'd be able to see a whole lot more, though, if you waited until morning."

Shad needed to explain.

"It might be that we'll want to pay 'em a visit before daybreak. Do me a favor and have everyone ready to ride just in case."

Abe understood. "Son, you can count on it," he said.

He knew that he could, for Abe was a veteran of trouble.

"We'll be here waitin' for your orders."

Shad made his way up the slope, dropping to the ground and proceeding on all fours when he neared the crest. At the top, he stopped and peered into the distance. A wind was blowing out of the south, but it had gentled with the coming of darkness. It carried the scent of prairie grasses as it brushed his face. He brought the field glasses to his eyes for a better view. The ranch lay spread out below him. Moonlight bathed the collection of weathered buildings, making the place look like an artist's painting. From this distance, all appeared to be quiet and serene, without a hint of the vicious murder that had taken place there such a short time before.

Shad noticed that a guard was posted close to the house, for he could see the glowing end of his cigarette. He caught a glimpse of another guard positioned farther out. A lantern was lit in the bunkhouse, and it illuminated the inside, a part of which he could see through the window. Half a dozen men sat around a table playing cards. That made eight outlaws for certain. But there was also the house to consider, and something about it puzzled him. First of all, there was a buckboard standing in front, and it hadn't been there at the time of the shooting. Not only that, the house was lit up like a saloon on a Saturday night. Whoever was inside wasn't in the least concerned about conserving kerosene.

While he watched, a man dressed in a broadcloth suit appeared in front of the window. He was pacing back and forth like he had something weighty on his mind. None of Rumbaugh's hands dressed that way, for a fact. It occurred to Shad that someone must have sent word to Craddock's nephew. If the nephew had hightailed it down to the ranch, he was in big trouble. They'd have to act fast, before Rumbaugh found out and ordered him killed.

He made his way back down the slope to where Abe and the others were waiting.

"What have you got to report?" Abe asked.

"It looks like Craddock's nephew has arrived. He's in the house."

"Then they must have sent a man to tell Rumbaugh about him. Most likely they're waiting to receive his orders before they do anything."

"That's what it looks like to me. If the nephew is going to have any chance at all, we'll have to get him out of there tonight."

The others, who were standing nearby, were listening.

"Tell us what to do," Slim Osborn said. "I'm prepared to go the distance, and I expect the other boys are, too."

Shad thought about how men like Osborn and Abe were worth more than a hundred men like Luke Crane.

"We'll attack under the cover of darkness," Shad replied. "If we work it right, the two guards won't see us. The others have their minds on a poker game. First we take out the guards. Then we hit the bunkhouse. We'll save the nephew for last. If he hasn't figured out what's going on already, we'll tell him. Then we'll take him with us and ride out of there.

"I guess you're not going to try to hold the ranch," said Abe.

"No. Rumbaugh and his outfit would starve us out. I think we'll have a better chance if he doesn't know where we are. We need to attack, then disappear, then attack again when he's not expecting it."

"I think you've got the right idea," Mc Nary said. "But what do we do with our two prisoners while we're on rescue detail?"

"Tie 'em up and leave 'em here. We'll take 'em with us when we're through, and if we can't, we'll leave 'em behind for their friends to find whenever they get around to it."

"Reckon that's the best we can do," he agreed.

Abe had been true to his word about seeing that everyone was ready. Shad was the last to mount up.

"We'll leave the spare horses and pick 'em up on our way out of here."

"Just a thought," Mc Nary said. "When we're

through with our business at the ranch, do you have a place in mind for us to go?"

"Yeah. But let's worry about getting the nephew out of there first."

He dared not tell them that they'd have to make a run for the mountains, just as he'd done the first time he'd escaped from the Craddock place.

They spread out and rode into the wind. Luck was with them in its direction, for the outlaws' horses would be unable to catch the scent of their own and sound an alarm. When they got as close as they dared, Shad, Abe, and Mc Nary dismounted and went the rest of the way on foot. The others waited behind for the signal. The three men moved stealthily forward. When Shad came to the perimeter guard, he paused. Rumbaugh's man looked like he was about half asleep. Without warning, Shad grabbed him from behind, his forearm coming up under the outlaw's chin. This served to cut off his air and, at the same time, it prevented him from crying out. With a quiet step, Mc Nary was beside him, stuffing a bandana into the outlaw's mouth. With a few deft movements, the man's hands were bound and he was effectively gagged. Shad and Mc Nary moved on to the other guard, who was unaware of what had happened. Abe stayed behind to watch the prisoner they'd just taken.

The second guard went down before he knew what had hit him. Now, they were free to rush the bunkhouse. Shad struck a match and held it in the air, a signal for the others to join them. Then, with the rest of his force backing him, he drew his revolver and kicked the bunkhouse door open. The crash startled the players. Chairs tipped over while cards and poker chips scattered in every direction.

"What the . . . ," one of them started in surprise.

"Hold it!" Shad ordered. "Put your hands in the air where I can see 'em real plain."

"You're a dead man, Wakefield," threatened the one standing nearest the door. "You too, Mc Nary."

It seemed the outlaws knew both of them.

"Shut up and listen," Mc Nary said.

Shad took a step forward, his gun aimed at a man clad only in his union suit.

"All of you, lay down on the floor, and put your hands behind your back while my men tie you up," he ordered. "If you behave yourselves, you might live through this."

"You'd better leave us and get out of here *pronto*," warned another outlaw. "We sent one of the boys to Rumbaugh's ranch with word that old man Craddock's heirs have arrived. You can bet your socks that he won't waste any time getting here, and he'll have some of the boys with him."

This was exactly what Shad had expected.

"Come with me," he said to Mc Nary.

They headed for the house at a run. Shad didn't pause before he hit the door with a flying kick. The man he'd seen framed in the window stood gaping in surprise. He was tall and thin, and he peered myopically through wire-rimmed glasses. Both his hands and voice betrayed his nervousness.

"What's the meaning of this?" he demanded to know.

"We're trying to save your life, if you're Craddock's nephew," Shad announced, glancing around the room to see if any of the outlaws were there.

"I'm Henry Craddock, but I don't know what you're talking about."

"I'm talking about murder. Your uncle was shot down, and the men on this ranch work for the killer. He wants this ranch, and Ben Craddock's heirs stand in his way. You, sir, stand in his way, and one bullet would remove you as an obstacle."

"Nonsense!" came a feminine voice from behind him.

He turned to find a woman posed in the doorway. She was smartly dressed in her riding outfit, and it showed she had the right curves in the right places. Her face was lovely too, if you discounted the disdain that marred it, but her eyes were what captured his attention. They were blue—but not the calm blue of the sky. They were bright with anger.

"This is my sister, Lucy," said Henry Craddock. "She's half owner of the ranch."

"Not for long, unless she's out of here before Jake Rumbaugh gets back with the rest of his gang."

Lucy Craddock swept on into the room.

"I don't know who you think you are," she said, "but I do know who killed my uncle. It was a snake named Shad Wakefield, and I intend to see that he hangs."

He should have expected her reaction.

"Plenty of no-accounts have been trying to hang Wakefield lately, and they ain't done it yet," Mc Nary said. "Which is a good thing, since he witnessed Rumbaugh putting a bullet into your uncle. Rumbaugh shot Wakefield's pardner because he saw the killing too."

"I don't believe you," she said. "Just who are you, anyway?"

"Name's Mc Nary, Ma'am, and I know Rumbaugh and Wakefield both. Rumbaugh is definitely the snake."

She turned to Shad. "Is that what you think, too?"

"Yes, Ma'am. I surely do."

"Then you don't know what you're talking about."

"Reckon I do, Miss Craddock. You see, I saw Jake Rumbaugh murder your uncle so he could get his hands on this ranch and its water. I also saw him gun down my partner, Charlie Pickett. And while it's not worth mentioning, I've got a scratch on the side of my head from a bullet that Rumbaugh meant to kill me with, 'cause he couldn't have me telling the truth about what had happened here."

Her face turned livid.

"You're Wakefield."

Her tone was so contemptuous that she was making him sorry he'd put himself out to save her hide.

"Yes, I'm Shad Wakefield," he said, "and I'm proud to bear the name. Now, if you want to live to claim your inheritance, you'd better mount up and ride, for Rumbaugh is on his way. When he gets here, he'll kill you."

Shad could see that he and Mc Nary had made some

progress convincing Henry, but Lucy wasn't buying any of it.

"If we have to take you out of here by force, we'll do it," he said.

A swift movement of her hand brought a derringer from a pocket in her skirt. It was aimed at Shad.

"Drop your guns!" she ordered. "Then back up against the wall. We're going to wait until Mr. Rumbaugh gets here. He'll know what to do with the likes of you."

Neither Shad nor Mc Nary moved to obey.

"You're making the biggest mistake of your life, Ma'am," Mc Nary warned her. "I'm telling you Rumbaugh's a killer without a conscience. I know, for I had the misfortune of working for him for a time. I've seen some of the things he's done."

"If you think you can lie your way out of this, you're mistaken. Mr. Rumbaugh is a fine man, and he's my uncle's best friend."

"Who fed you that line?" Shad asked.

"The men who worked for my uncle."

"If you're talking about the ones in the bunkhouse, they're outlaws and they work for Rumbaugh."

Henry Craddock stepped closer to his sister.

"Lucy, I think these men are telling the truth."

She glared at him.

"Then you're simple-minded."

"No, I'm not. I overheard a couple of them talking awhile ago, and it's worried me ever since. One of them said that you were a beautiful woman, and it was a cryin' shame that you were going to have to die so young. They moved on then, but it sounded like they knew it was going to happen."

"If you stay here any longer," Shad warned, "you can bet on it."

He could see that nothing they'd said had changed her mind.

"We're all going to stay right here until Mr. Rumbaugh and his men arrive. You can tell your lies to him then."

"By then, it'll be too late for all of us," Shad said.

Henry Craddock was convinced. Two quick steps took him close enough to grab the derringer from his sister's grasp.

"Henry, you fool!" she cried. "Now they'll probably kill us."

"Oh, shut up, Lucy."

He turned to Shad. "Wakefield, I'd be much obliged if you could get us out of this mess, somehow."

"I'll scream for help," Lucy threatened.

"Then go ahead and scream," Shad invited.

While she was trying to make up her mind whether or not to do it, he grabbed her and dragged her from the house. She struggled all the way.

Abe and Kaminski saddled a couple of horses for the Craddocks.

"Afraid there's no sidesaddle, Ma'am," Abe apologized. "You'll just have to ride the other way."

Shad was still hanging on to her, pinning her arms to her sides. She was still struggling and calling him names, but she stopped long enough to address Abe.

"I won't do it. I'm not leaving here."

"Oh, you're leaving here," Shad told her. "You're leaving here if I have to tie you up like a sack of potatoes and toss you over the saddle."

He was glad to see that his threat did the trick. She appeared to calm down a little. Then she climbed into the saddle and rode like a man. They left all of the outlaws bound and shut up in the bunkhouse. Whether or not they'd get loose before their boss arrived and found them like that was something he didn't care to bet on.

They rode back to where they'd made camp. But they stayed only long enough to retrieve their spare horses and the two prisoners. Then, with Shad in the lead, they headed for the mountains that had sheltered him before. In a little while it would be daylight. He wanted to put as much distance between himself and the Craddock ranch as possible while they still had darkness for cover.

He had no doubt that Rumbaugh and his men would soon be on his trail. The outlaw would have to kill Shad, and he'd have to kill the Craddocks too, no matter how young and pretty Lucy was. The fact that she was a woman wouldn't save her, either. In fact, it'd be a massacre if Rumbaugh got his way, for he couldn't afford to let any of them live to tell what they knew. The outlaw had put everything on the line, and it was way too late for him to back down, even if backing down had ever been in his thinking.

Shad was concerned about Cletus Osborn's bum leg and Loftis's banged-up head, but both of them were keeping up with the rest, and they were doing their jobs. He felt a kind of pride in the men who'd chosen to ride with him. But that pride intensified the shame he felt for his former boss. He wondered if Crane was still out looking for him with a hanging rope in one hand. Knowing the man's bullheaded tenacity, he'd guess that he was.

Not long after sunup, they stopped to change horses. Lucy climbed down and walked over to him.

"I hope you know that kidnapping is against the law," she said, looking up at him, her face a picture of defiance.

"What difference do you think that would that make to the cold-blooded killer you claim that I am?"

Her brother came up beside her.

"Leave him be, Lucy. He's trying to save our lives."

She made an unladylike snort, turned on her heel, and stalked away.

"She'll come around," Henry said.

At the moment Shad had more important things to worry about than Lucy Craddock's contempt. They had to get to the mountains, for there was no protection on the plains.

There was no way of telling how much of a head start they had on the outlaws, but he figured it was only a matter of hours. Once in the mountains, though, it would be easier to cover their trail. He figured that if he could work it right, he might be able to turn the tables on Rumbaugh and his gunmen. Anyway, he had a few tricks up his sleeve that he wanted to try. If those tricks worked, it might buy them some time and give them at least half a chance.

Chapter Seven

For hours Shad and his allies rode across the plains toward the mountains, with their prisoners and the Craddocks in tow. When they reached the foothills Shad felt a strong sense of relief. They were less vulnerable here than on the flat land.

From time to time, he'd caught glimpses of Lucy Craddock eying the prisoners, and he could almost read her thoughts. Given the chance, he wouldn't put it past her to try to free them, in spite of the hard truths she'd been told. She believed only what it pleased her to believe, no matter how dangerous and absurd. He wouldn't argue the point that she was a beautiful woman, but she was a hardheaded know-it-all, and she was apt to get a lot of good men killed.

He was breaking his own trail as he led the climb from the lower elevations. When they reached a place that overlooked the wide, open spaces below, he signaled the others to stop.

"Wait here," he said. "I'd better have a look."

While the others waited, concealed among the trees, he crawled out onto the narrow ledge with the field glasses in one hand. The ledge's height gave him an excellent vantage point. The plains spread out below him to the horizon, while a mesa towered above them miles away. The prairie grasses rippled in the wind. It looked like a huge grass ocean that spread across the land as far as he could see. It didn't take him long to spot the moving cloud of dust in the distance. It was being raised by horses that were being ridden hard. They were still too far away and the dust was too thick for him to make out the individual riders. But there was no doubt about it, they were headed straight toward the mountain.

He hadn't anticipated having to rescue Craddock's niece and nephew from the bad spot they'd gotten themselves into. It was pure dumb luck that he and the others had arrived before it was too late. Maybe it was still too late for any of them, but at least they had a fighting chance now. He moved back from the ledge and returned to where the others were waiting.

"I spotted Rumbaugh and his outfit," he announced. "They're headed this way."

A triumphant look spread across Lucy Craddock's face.

"He's coming to rescue Henry and me. I hope that Mr. Rumbaugh makes all of you sorry that you were ever born."

Abe scowled like he'd had his fill of her smart mouth. Usually, he appeared grandfatherly, but he sure didn't appear grandfatherly now. He stepped up in front of her and looked her right in the eye so she'd know that he meant business.

"You'd better not hope that, Ma'am, for all that's standing between you and a bullet, and maybe something that's even worse, is Shad Wakefield and the rest of us who've put our lives on the line with him. Kaminski, here, got his home burned down by Rumbaugh's outlaws, and they killed his two cowhands. Trujillo and Joe Beale, over there, had to take to the high grass to keep from getting shot when Rumbaugh's men raided Joe's ranch and stole all of his livestock. Rumbaugh, himself, shot down Charlie Pickett, who was a good man with the bad luck to witness your uncle's murder. Make no mistake, young lady, Jake Rumbaugh wants the Box C bad enough to kill for it. Now that you and your brother stand in the way of what he wants, he's out to kill you, too."

She looked shaken at his speech, but unconvinced.

"He's right, Lucy," said her brother, peering at her through his spectacles. "Uncle Ben wrote me that there was a big rancher from the East that was giving him a lot of trouble. Said he didn't want me to worry you about it, so I didn't. But this has been going on for quite awhile."

She stamped her foot. "Why didn't you tell me this before?" she demanded to know.

"I've just told you, I didn't do it before because he asked me not to."

The woman had been angry ever since Shad had first seen her, but now she was downright livid. This time Henry was her target.

"You made all that up just now in order to get me to believe those same obvious lies that you believe."

"No. I'm telling the truth, Lucy. These men are trying mightily to save your silly, ungrateful life."

Shad figured it was about time for the sparks to fly.

"Don't you ever speak to me like that again, Henry. If Mr. Rumbaugh manages to save us from these outlaws, I've got half a mind to sell my part of the ranch just so I never have to see you again."

From the look on Henry's face, it was plain he was starting to think that not seeing Lucy wasn't such a bad deal.

"We've got to get a move on," Shad warned. "Time's running short."

Lucy decided to shut up, and they all fell into line behind him.

Breaking a new trail through the mountain wilderness was painstakingly slow. He was leading them up to where the cover was thicker, where it would be hard for the outlaws to track them. He recalled a place that he'd spotted when he was trying to get away from Rumbaugh before. If he could find it again, it would offer them a defensible position with an escape route. He didn't have it all worked out yet, but one thing he knew for certain, he had more to worry about than survival. If Rumbaugh and his gunmen were to leave the mountain victorious, they would continue to terrorize the area ranchers. What's more, there would be no one around with the power to stop them.

Shad noticed a faint trail crossing his own at an angle. It, too, led upward. Leading the others, he followed the ancient pathway. At this height, the air smelled fresh and cool, and the wind played gently through the pine needles. The whispering windsong was soothing to the soul. Here in the midst of the wilderness, the meanness that was taking place on the plains seemed a long way off. But he was aware that there were dangers here, as well.

The long hours of wakefulness were starting to get to him, and he yearned for a few hours of uninterrupted sleep. But sleep was a luxury he couldn't afford, at least not for awhile. He struggled to stay alert.

With so many horses in their outfit, it was difficult to cover their tracks completely. But they did what they could to make it hard for the outlaws to follow them. When they came to a stretch of bare rock, they rode across it, leaving no prints or other signs of their passing. It would slow Rumbaugh down and he would have to look for the place where their tracks resumed. After they left the rock surface, they doubled back for a time before taking up the old trail again. It followed the curve of the mountain toward the south.

Shad was riding a little ahead of the others, and he turned back to check on them. The injured ones were coming along fine, better than he'd dared to hope. Henry Craddock, on the other hand, looked like he wished he'd never left Denver City. His sister's face was cold and angry as she rode beside him. Shad had never seen anyone so hostile toward the man who'd saved her from certain death. Neither had he seen anyone so eager to embrace her would-be murderer. It took all kinds, he supposed.

He turned and went on. After a time, they arrived at the stream he'd discovered while on foot that first night on the mountainside. Shad urged the sorrel into the edge of the current. It was still as cold and swift in its downhill tumble as he remembered. The others followed him, with Mc Nary and Abe keeping a close watch on the prisoners, as well as the Craddocks. Kaminski and the Osborns rode at the back, for they were bringing along the spare horses on lead ropes. Abe left the prisoners in Mc Nary's custody and rode ahead to catch up with Shad.

"Would you be looking for anything in particular?" Abe asked in a low voice that couldn't be heard by the ones who were following.

"I'm looking for a safe place for the rest of you to stay, while I go back and have some fun with Rumbaugh and his outfit."

Abe pretended dismay.

"What, and leave me and the rest of your friends out of the game?"

"Well, I need you and the others to take care of all the outlaws that I can't handle. Besides, the rest of you have to guard the prisoners, the horses, and that woman."

Abe chuckled. "The one that has the misfortune of guarding Miss Craddock might have the hardest job of all."

Shad didn't disagree with him.

Another few minutes, and they left the spring and headed south again. Shad had a feeling from the looks of things that he was getting close to the shelter he was searching for. When at last he found it, the place was just as he remembered seeing it. The wind-eroded hollow could just barely be called a cave. It was shallow, but wide enough to shelter all of them and the horses too. There were young pines and a tangle of underbrush growing up close to it, almost concealing the entrance from certain angles. The trees and brush would serve to provide cover. There was also a channel that had washed down one side from years of spring flooding. If a man hunkered down in it, he'd be completely hidden while using it as an escape route. The escape route was a safety precaution that his father had taught him years before.

"Son, never let yourself get trapped," he'd said. "Make certain you have a way to get out when you need to, even if you have to dig it yourself with a teaspoon."

He'd said those words more than a decade ago, and they were so impressed on Shad's mind that it was as if he'd uttered them the week before.

"This is it," he told the others as he reined up before the cave. "Put the horses inside, store the supplies, and try to get some rest 'cause you're going to need it."

Abe looked the place over with approval.

"This is probably the best you could hope to do," he said. "Now what?"

"While somebody else guards the prisoners and

keeps watch, I'm going to try to get an hour or so of sleep."

"Good idea. We've got that much time. Probably more. Not to mention that you're about to drop in your tracks, whether you've got the time or not."

"I'm counting on you to wake me."

Abe nodded his assurance.

Shad spread his bedroll at one end of the cave and crawled into it, glad to finally be getting some rest. He was still alert enough to notice that Lucy Craddock had positioned herself as far away from him as she could get. That suited him just fine. Some people were born hardheaded, and she was as hardheaded as they come. He figured that if she lived long enough, life would teach her some necessary lessons. After that last thought, sleep came, while he was too tired to welcome it.

He awoke suddenly to find Abe shaking his shoulder. It was late evening, and already there was a chill in the air.

"Any sign of Rumbaugh?" he asked.

"Nope. Not yet. But I've got a feeling that him and the rest of his bunch ain't all that far away. It's one of them feelings that I've learned to trust."

"I believe that it's called instinct," Shad said as he climbed out of the bedroll and stretched his muscles. "What's more, I expect you're right."

"I thought you might want some grub before you left."

Abe handed Shad a cup of hot coffee and a couple of biscuits, along with a few pieces of dried apple.

"Better savor it, 'cause this is the last of the coffee. I made 'em douse the fire. Can't risk it, any longer."

It had been a long time since Shad had eaten, and the apple pieces and hard biscuits, washed down with strong coffee, helped to stop the rumbling in his stomach, even though they didn't fill him up.

"Whilst you was asleep, I sent Mc Nary down the slope a little ways to keep a lookout. Didn't figure it'd hurt none to have some warning."

"Good idea, *amigo*."

He wondered if Mc Nary was as shy on sleep as he had been. Maybe he didn't need as much, or maybe he was managing to ignore the need.

He pulled on his jacket in order to ward off the bone-chilling cold that was already beginning to settle in.

"Abe, make sure that everyone is armed and alert, excepting those that ought not to be armed, of course. Better keep a close watch on the prisoners."

Osborn overheard what he'd said.

"Are you goin' off by yourself too?"

"I figured on it. I can't let Rumbaugh get too comfortable. It's time for him to be worried a little."

"I'll sure throw in with you, there."

"Just be careful," warned Abe. "Don't ever underestimate that varmint."

Shad didn't intend to. He checked the Army Colt that he'd bought in St. Louis, and slung his rifle over his shoulder. He also made sure he had plenty of rounds of ammunition. When a wise man goes into battle, he goes prepared.

Lucy Craddock was seated apart from the others, gazing out on the wilderness. She was pretending that the likes of Shad Wakefield didn't exist. That was all right with him, but he didn't want her making any mischief, either.

"Watch her," he whispered to Abe. "I wouldn't put it past that fool woman to try something dangerous."

Abe nodded.

"It's a hard thing to say about a lady," he said, "but I think she deserves the likes of Rumbaugh—almost."

Shad thought she almost did too. But not quite.

Without further delay, he slipped through the underbrush and the pines, leading the line-back dun. Mc Nary was keeping himself well hidden, for Shad saw no sign of him. When he was a little distance away from the shelter, he climbed into the saddle and began to make his way downward. This time it was different from the last time he'd gone down the mountain. This time he wasn't running for his life like a wounded animal. His role had changed. He was the hunter, now, not the quarry.

Chapter Eight

Above him, the Evening Star dominated a sky that was sprinkled with lesser lights. Night had descended, and Shad felt at home in the night. But under the best of conditions the mountain could be treacherous, and darkness wasn't the best of conditions. Fortunately, this would hold true for the outlaws as much as for himself. In addition, he would have the advantage of cover and surprise whenever he found them. How he'd use this advantage, he didn't yet know.

In his solitude, thoughts of his father filled his mind. He realized that he'd been thinking of Dunham Wakefield a lot in recent days. Shad wondered what a man like his father would have done in this situation. He couldn't say for sure, but he had no doubt that in some way he would be fighting back, not running away. But then, Shad wasn't running either. Beginning with the

96

rescue of the Craddocks, he was challenging Rumbaugh in a way the outlaw couldn't ignore. But with fewer men to back him up, not to mention the cantankerous woman he was stuck with, he simply had to be a little smarter and a lot more cautious about how he proceeded.

He'd never had any doubt that the outlaws would track them into the foothills. But after that, it would be harder for them to read the sign. At least, they'd be slowed down a little, and now the darkness would cost Rumbaugh even more time.

Shad carefully worked his way downward at an angle that would intersect the trail that Rumbaugh would most likely be following. His senses were alert for any unusual sounds or movement. Still, he was startled when he heard a sharp report. It had come from off to his right, and it sounded as if an animal or a human had stepped on a fallen branch, snapping it under their weight. He stopped, and his hand went to the .44 at his hip. For a time he waited, listening for anything that would betray an enemy. The minutes passed, but he heard nothing more than a few night sounds. Still, he had a gut feeling that someone had been close by, for he'd sensed a human presence. That presence either hadn't seen him, or it hadn't wanted to be seen. He dismounted, and with his gun drawn he eased his way over to where he'd heard the noise. There was no sign of anyone. Shad went back to the dun and moved on, keeping to the deepest shadows of the pines.

The way the outlaws had been hightailing it toward the mountain meant they'd most likely be somewhere on the slope by now. His plan was to intercept them before they discovered the cave and attacked. He would do his best to worry them and keep them off balance.

The darkness would surely have forced them to stop and make camp by now, and this was in his favor. He had only to locate the camp. He pressed forward, still convinced that someone had been close by when that branch had snapped. This concerned him. But the knowledge that someone might be out there in the darkness would serve to keep him wary.

Once, in a steep place, the dun dislodged a rock with its hoof. The rock went tumbling, dislodging smaller rocks in its descent. Shad listened in dismay at what sounded to him like an avalanche in the quiet of the night. At last the slide subsided, leaving only the rustling of pine needles.

"You've got to be more careful, boy," he warned the big horse. "I can't have you breaking a leg."

He noticed that being the hunter took almost as steep a toll on a man's nerves as being the hunted. He was grateful for those few hours of sleep that he'd gotten before he left the cave. The night was apt to be a long one, and he would need his wits about him.

In the distance, he could hear the downhill rushing of a stream. He rode closer before he stopped again to listen. There was no sign or sound of Rumbaugh and his bunch. Still, he had the feeling that they were somewhere below. Most likely, they were camped somewhere close to the trail that he'd broken on his ascent.

From time to time, he checked his back trail. Another lesson that he'd learned early was that it was better to be overly cautious than to risk dying because of carelessness. It could have been an Indian that had snapped the branch. Maybe a Kiowa or a Ute. But he doubted if a member of either tribe would have been so careless. He discounted the possibility that it had been one of Rumbaugh's men. That left only those from his own camp, which didn't seem logical. Maybe it was just an animal, after all, he told himself. Perhaps an elk. That answer almost satisfied him, and he deliberately dismissed the noise from his mind.

There were times when he couldn't see the sky because of the canopy formed by the dense forest; but whenever he could catch glimpses of the constellations, they were sliding relentlessly across the heavens. He was aware that there was only a few hours of darkness left. He rode as fast as he dared, which wasn't fast at all, since much of the time he had to pick his way carefully downward. All the while, he was forced to balance recklessness with caution, for a lot depended on the outcome of this night's work.

Even more time had elapsed when he spotted the embers of a campfire. Quietly he dismounted and left the dun ground-tethered at a safe distance. Then he donned the soft moccasins that he'd brought with him and moved forward toward the camp. The smell of the horses in the remuda was strong. Most of the outlaws were asleep in their bedrolls, but two guards had been posted. It seemed that Rumbaugh was never satisfied with only one. Shad noticed something else, as well.

One of the sleeping men had a bandanna tied across his mouth, and it looked as though his hands were bound. From what he could make out, it appeared that Cory Beale's plan had failed, for Cory was now Rumbaugh's prisoner.

Shad felt a resurgence of anger, and it was directed at the trussed-up kid in the outlaw's camp. If it weren't for Cory's impetuousness, Lucy Craddock's know-it-all arrogance, and Luke Crane's hardheaded disloyalty, his task would have been a whole lot easier. But things were the way they were, not the way he preferred them to be. He had to work with reality, no matter how difficult it was.

What he needed in order to free Cory was a diversion, so he went about the business of creating one. He slipped the knife from his belt and moved in closer to the camp. It was plain that the guards weren't expecting trouble. After all, they were the predators, not the game. They both looked bored and half asleep. The trouble was, Cory looked like he was asleep too. His face—what Shad could see of it—was bruised and swollen. Shad got as close as he could without leaving his cover. Then he bent down and gathered a handful of pebbles. When the guards were looking the other way, Shad tossed a pebble. It hit its mark, which was Cory's head. The kid stirred in his sleep. Shad had time to throw another before one of the guards glanced over to check the prisoner. When he turned away, Shad resumed the pelting. Cory turned his head to see where the barrage was coming from and spotted Shad.

Shad put his finger to his lips before he stepped back into the deeper cover of the forest.

With Cory alert now, he could create his diversion. There was only the moon, a few stars that weren't hidden by branches, and some dying embers to shed light. He crept along in a roundabout way toward the remuda. A slight breeze was blowing, and Shad moved in against it, so it would blow his human smell away from the horses. The animals remained quiet, occasionally flicking their tails. His presence didn't disturb them, and with a few quick slashes of the knife, he set them free. He slapped the nearest one on the rump and howled at the top of his lungs. The startled horses lunged forward. At the same time, he dived for cover.

The outlaws piled out of their bedrolls like they'd found rattlers inside. There was a lot of confusion and yelling. One of the guards fired into the air, and this caused the horses to run even faster. Since being stranded afoot put an end to their manhunt, they pulled on their boots and took off after their fleeing mounts. Shad moved in and yanked the bandanna from Cory's mouth. With a slash of the knife, he freed his legs. Cory grabbed his boots and half ran, half stumbled into the woods after his benefactor.

"Come on, Beale" he urged. "They'll be after us as soon as they catch their horses."

"I'm right behind you."

When they reached the place where he'd left the dun, Shad paused to slash the piggin' strings that bound Cory's wrists. It was plain that he'd taken a beating.

"Thanks for the rescue," he said. "I guess there's not much point in admitting to you that I was dead wrong."

"Nope," Shad agreed. "Just listen the next time somebody tries to tell you something. It might turn out to save your hide. Now, climb up on the dun and we'll ride double."

Shad didn't like to make the dun carry a double load, but there simply wasn't any alternative. Cory got his boots on in record time and did what he was told.

"You okay?" he asked when Cory was seated.

"I guess so. They roughed me up pretty good. Rumbaugh never quite believed that I'd walked away from a sizeable ranch to work for him for the wages of a cowhand. I told him that I was at odds with Uncle Joe, and that I wanted to strike out on my own. But when we got to the Craddock place, his trust just disappeared. He was mad about what happened and he took it out on me."

"Nice fellow," Shad said sarcastically.

"He's cold, Shad. I don't think he's got a human feeling inside him."

"Well, maybe he's got a couple of the bad ones. But killing somebody sure doesn't seem to bother him. At least not so you'd notice."

"That's the truth of it. Where are we going?"

"I'm taking you up to where the others are camped. Maybe Abe can help you. I know for sure that your uncle is going to be glad to see you."

"There's a problem with that," Cory said, his voice wavering.

"Are you worried about Loftis?"

"Yeah. It's going to be hard enough to face my uncle, but Loftis is going to wring my neck."

"After what you did to him, I'd be pleased to hold your neck for him to wring."

But truth to tell, Shad figured the kid had paid for his hardheadedness, as well as for what he'd done to Loftis. He imagined that even Loftis would agree.

He nudged the dun in the sides. They were climbing, and the going was slower with the double load. They had to stop often to rest.

During one of the stops, Cory leaned against a tree, holding his side.

"You okay?" Shad asked, realizing that it was a foolish question for someone in Cory's hurt condition.

"I've felt better," he said

"Then rest awhile before we go on."

Cory bent his knees and slid into a sitting position.

"You know something, Shad, when Rumbaugh got to the Craddock place and found his men tied up in the bunkhouse and the Craddocks gone, he went a little crazy."

"How do you mean?"

"He got a real strange look on his face and pulled his gun. Then he demanded to know which one of 'em was responsible. Of course, nobody volunteered. Then he stomped and hollered 'til I thought he was going to have some kind of spell and maybe drop dead. I guess most of us hoped that he would drop dead. His men are afraid of him, and none of 'em are angels, themselves. Most of 'em are pretty tough *hombres*, in fact. Then he ordered a couple of his men to hold me while he proceeded to beat me up."

Shad tried to picture Rumbaugh "stomping and hollering" and it didn't take much imagination. He could also see him beating up Cory without giving him a chance to defend himself. This was just one more score that Shad had to settle with the killer of his partner.

"I'd like to get my hands on that rattlesnake in a fair fight," Cory said. "Maybe I'd still get beat up, but I could make him hurt plenty, and that's something he's not used to."

"You're not in any shape to be thinking of a fist-fight right now. But don't worry. One way or another Rumbaugh is going to get what's coming to him."

"What you ought to know," Cory went on, "is that when Rumbaugh finds where the Craddocks and the rest of us are hiding, he's sure to go on another rampage. I don't think he intends to let any of us live."

"I figured that's how it'd be if he gets his way. From his point of view, he can't afford to let any of us live. A mass killing wouldn't trouble him overmuch either. Remember, I saw him gun down two people, and one of 'em was an old man who wasn't armed. Afterward, he chased me all over this bloomin' mountain. A man who's crazy with greed and wild for power is a tough enemy to go up against."

With great effort, Cory pushed himself upright until he was standing without the aid of the tree trunk.

"We'd better get to wherever it is we're going and warn the others," he said, "for as soon as the outlaws round up their horses they'll be coming for us. Rumbaugh will be in a rage, and he won't wait around for anything."

Shad had no doubt the kid was right.

"Come on, then, if you can manage."

"Mind if I join you?" a voice called from nearby.

He recognized it as belonging to Mc Nary.

"You followed me," Shad said, more a statement of fact than an accusation.

Mc Nary rode up.

"I saw you leave the cave and I couldn't let you go down there alone, so I followed you just in case. You might have gotten into trouble, and I didn't want to miss out on all the fun."

"It was you that broke that branch."

"Yeah. Careless of me, but it was dark. By the way, that was a clever rescue you pulled off. Couldn't have done it better myself."

"Well thanks, Mc Nary. It's a good thing to know that if I'd needed your help you'd have been there."

"No thanks are necessary. As it turned out, you did just fine on your own."

"I had some luck. But we need to get Cory back to the cave. He could stand some patching up."

"Rumbaugh do that?"

"Yeah," Cory said. "I figure I owe him."

"We all do," Mc Nary agreed, and Shad figured he was remembering the pistol whipping that Rumbaugh had administered.

While the three of them rode on together, a subtle change took place overhead. The sky started to lighten.

It wasn't long before daylight was filtering down through the branches, making it easier for them to pick their way through the wilderness. But then it would make things easier for Rumbaugh's outfit, too.

When at last they approached the cave, Trujillo stepped out from behind some scrub. His rifle barrel rested in the crook of his arm. The Beales' cowhand was a wiry fellow without an extra ounce of flesh on his bones. But he was a man to be reckoned with; you could tell it by the look in his eyes.

"Señor Cory, what did they do to you?" Trujillo asked.

Cory groaned as he slid from the back of the dun.

"Rumbaugh decided to use me for his punching bag, but he didn't want to take any chances that I might hit back. He ordered a couple of his men to hold me while he did his dirty work."

"That *hombre* is filth," Trujillo said as he spat on the ground.

Shad dismounted.

"Glad to see you're guarding the approach, Trujillo. Rumbaugh and his men lost track of their horses for awhile, but I expect that as soon as they find 'em again they'll be coming up here to pay us a visit."

Trujillo got an odd expression on his face.

"Is something wrong?" Shad asked. "I mean is something wrong that I don't already know about?"

"I think it's best that you take Señor Cory to his uncle. He will tell you everything that's happened."

With a sense of foreboding, Shad took up the reins

of the dun and followed Cory through the brush to the cave.

The others heard them coming, and Joe Beale hurried over and threw his arm around his nephew's shoulder, helping him into their camp.

"I never expected to see you alive again, son," he said. "It looks to me like they didn't believe your story."

"It was a fool thing I did, running off like that. I'm real sorry about the way I treated Loftis, too."

"Then you'd better go and tell him, yourself."

Loftis emerged from the back of the cave and looked his assailant over.

"It appears like you've had yourself some trouble," he said.

"Yeah, but it's my own fault. I'm sorry I hit you the way I did."

"Can't say it didn't hurt, but there's no point in dwelling on it."

During their exchange, Shad glanced around the hideout. It looked different to him. It seemed bigger and emptier, somehow. Then it struck him. The Craddock woman and both of the prisoners were gone.

"Where's your sister?" he asked Henry Craddock.

Craddock looked ashamed.

"Somehow she managed to free the outlaws. Then she ran off with them."

So that was what Trujillo had been reluctant to tell him.

"How in blazes could she do that with all of you right here watching her?"

Craddock shifted his weight from one foot to the other in embarrassment, and peered over his spectacles.

"Lucy is resourceful. She always has been. Whatever it is that she wants to do, she finds a way to do it."

"Those were Rumbaugh's men that she let loose, and your sister is high on the list of people that Rumbaugh intends to kill."

Craddock's expression turned to one of alarm.

"Surely he wouldn't harm a woman!"

Abe spoke up from where he'd been watching and listening.

"A rattlesnake like Rumbaugh don't care a whit about whether he's killing a woman, a preacher, a child, or his own kinfolk."

"I should have tried to stop her," Craddock said to himself in a barely audible voice.

Shad stepped forward and grabbed him by the shirt front.

"You mean to say that you knew she was going to take off with them?" he asked in disbelief. "And you didn't say a word or try to stop her?"

"No, no," he protested, "I didn't know, not really. But I was sure she wasn't convinced that you were okay, or that Rumbaugh was a killer. That being the case, Lucy wouldn't have stood by very long without doing something to interfere."

Shad had no regard for Lucy Craddock, but he had a sinking feeling in the pit of his stomach that she had willfully ridden to her death.

"How did it happen?" he asked.

"She must have slipped around and cut their bonds when nobody was paying any particular attention," Abe explained. "Then in the night, when everyone was asleep, they snuck out past the guard."

"That's about the size of it," Joe Beale agreed.

"Then I don't guess there's any point in asking if they're armed."

"Nope," Abe said. "They're armed, and it's a good thing the rest of us was sleeping with our weapons practically in our hands or they'd most likely have took 'em. Probably would have shot us too, if they hadn't been afraid the woman would have shot them for doing it. Three of our horses are gone too."

Under his breath, Shad uttered a curse. He sincerely wished that Lucy Craddock had stayed up in Denver City where a woman like her belonged. But, unfortunately, wishing wouldn't change a thing.

"Son, tell us what you found down there at that outlaw camp when you fetched Cory back," said Abe.

"There must be a dozen of 'em. Rumbaugh appears to have brought the ones from the Craddock place as well as some from the Lazy R. They're well armed too. I scattered their horses and got Cory out of their camp. I don't know how much time that bought us, but they'll be combing this mountain once they have their horses rounded up."

"What are we going to do?" Craddock asked, his voice strained. "We have to do something to help Lucy."

Shad had been thinking about how they were going

to deal with Rumbaugh for a long time, but the new circumstances altered things a little.

"We've got almost as many men as Rumbaugh has," he said. "We need to use that to our advantage. My pa used to tell me that oft times the best defense is a good attack. That's what we're going to do. We're going to move out of here and attack. The outlaws aren't going to have it all their own way anymore."

"But what about Lucy?" Craddock insisted.

Shad held back from telling the man what he thought about his sister. In spite of everything they had said and done, she'd headed straight for the man who intended to kill her and her brother. Still, he couldn't help but feel pity for her, and especially for Henry Craddock, who obviously cared about her.

"We've got to get her away from Rumbaugh before he kills her," he said.

What Shad left unsaid was how little hope he held out for her rescue. Given Rumbaugh's violent temper, along with his need to get rid of the Craddock heirs, the outlaw wasn't apt to waste any time.

He dragged his saddle from the dun and threw it over the sorrel's back. He tightened the cinch, and then switched his saddlebags. Lastly, he made sure that both his .44 and his Winchester were loaded. When he was finished, Abe handed him a cup of coffee and a strip of jerky.

"You're going to need something to sustain you," he said.

It appeared that Abe had decided to risk a small fire. Shad swallowed the hot coffee as quickly as he could tolerate it, and let it warm his insides. Then he chewed hungrily on the jerky. He'd been on short rations for so long that he was almost getting used to them. Cory was given the same fare and was making the best of it. While they were eating, the others finished packing and began mounting up. He was concerned that Loftis and Cletus weren't in very good shape. But then, Cory was in worse shape than either one of them. They'd have to move out regardless, for they dared not leave anyone behind. The prisoners and Lucy Craddock all knew precisely where the cave was located, and that meant Rumbaugh would soon know, as well. Shad took one last swallow of coffee and climbed into the saddle.

"Think we can trail the girl?" Mc Nary asked.

Shad figured that the prisoners had a pretty fair idea about where their boss would be, and they'd take Lucy Craddock straight to him. He, too, had a fair idea of where their boss would be. Following her tracks wouldn't even be necessary.

"Yeah, I think we can trail her," he said.

Chapter Nine

Lucy Craddock was beginning to wonder if maybe she had made a mistake. The uncertainty she was starting to feel was disquieting to say the least. Self-doubt was something she rarely experienced, and she didn't like it one little bit.

Her first misgiving had come when the man with the squeaky voice had told her to shut up. That was no way to talk to a lady, especially one who'd just helped you escape your captors. The man was an ingrate. The one he called Darby was equally rude and nasty, once they had gotten well away from the cave and any possibility of help. She intended to make sure that Mr. Rumbaugh heard about the unconscionable way they'd treated her. No doubt, he'd give them a good dressing-down and then fire them on the spot. From what she'd been told, she imagined that he was an impressive man who required good behavior from the inferior types who served him. The thought of watching their public humiliation gave her a measure of satisfaction.

"Come on, woman," Darby ordered. "Quit your straggling. We've still got a long ways to go and not much time left."

Lucy hated being addressed that way, but she did the uncustomary. She bit back a sharp retort. It wasn't that she was afraid, she told herself. It's just that this awful wilderness was no place to start an altercation. She was certain that she couldn't find her way back to the others alone, and she didn't know where to find Mr. Rumbaugh. She'd bide her time. Those two uncouth saddle bums would get their comeuppance soon enough. She was willing to settle for that. Besides, it was worth all that she was going through to see Wakefield hang. Henry had been stupid enough to believe his lies, and the lies of the rest of his gang, but Henry had never been very bright. Without her to push him and guide him, her brother would never have amounted to anything at all. It was thanks to her efforts that Henry had been able to get a position as a bank clerk. It was also due to her skillful matchmaking that he was almost engaged to the bank president's daughter. Lucy was pleased that news of their inheritance would help to speed things along. After all, Henry was an affluent landowner now, and a worthy husband for the daughter of one of Denver City's finest families.

From the first moment she'd heard about the inheritance, she'd been making plans. As soon as possible, they'd hire someone to run the ranch, allowing them to return to the amenities of the city. Then after Henry's marriage, the three of them would move into a fine home befitting their position. Those socially prominent women who'd snubbed all her overtures would soon be vying for invitations to her teas and receptions. The thought was so pleasant that it made her feel better in spite of her present circumstances. It also gave her the courage to act.

Little by little, she lagged behind the two men. She wanted to distance herself and still have them where she could see them, even though they were only dark silhouettes in the dark night. At the same time, they couldn't see her without turning. That way she could follow them to Mr. Rumbaugh without having to endure their company. Unfortunately, it wasn't long before the one called Darby noticed what she was doing.

"Gooch, get that woman up here where we can keep an eye on her," he ordered.

The man with the squeaky voice dropped back and grabbed the reins from her hand. Then with a sharp jerk, he pulled her toward him.

"Get your hands off!" she shouted, not caring who heard.

When she was ordered to shut up for the second time, she leaned over and slapped him hard across his face. The sound of the blow reverberated. Then, before she knew what was happening, Gooch gripped her by the wrists and dragged her off the horse. Darby rode back to assist him.

Lucy struggled and yelled threats at them as they bound her with rope. In the midst of her tirade, one of them stuffed a filthy rag into her mouth and secured it. Next, she was hoisted and thrown over the horse like a sack of grain. It was exactly what that killer, Wakefield, had threatened to do, back at her uncle's ranch. Mr. Rumbaugh was going to hear about this. No doubt he'd horsewhip the two scoundrels who'd failed to treat her in a respectful manner. But for now, she'd have to endure even this.

The downhill ride was uncomfortable in the extreme. She was bounced and jostled unmercifully, and there was no way she could brace herself. Her anger quickly turned to rage, and rage changed to fear and hopelessness. *Could it be that Wakefield and the others had been telling the truth?* For awhile she dared not contemplate the answer. When she did, she became more frightened than she'd ever thought possible. If what those men had said about Mr. Rumbaugh was true, then he would surely kill her. What's more, there seemed to be nothing she could do to save herself.

"Don't this side of the mountain seem a lot more peaceful, now?" Gooch asked his partner.

"It surely does. I expect Rumbaugh's going to get his ear full, though, whenever he pulls out that gag."

"Well, he didn't have any trouble shutting her uncle up, so I don't reckon he'll have any trouble shutting this one up, either."

Lucy's last hope vanished with that admission. How

could she have misjudged everyone so terribly? She was always right, or almost always. And the times she was wrong were easily ignored and forgotten. But this was different. She feared that this mistake was going to cost her her life.

Another thought came to her. Maybe this was all a joke meant to scare her. They were the kind of men who'd do such a thing. Maybe when they got to Mr. Rumbaugh, they'd untie her and tell her it was all just a prank, and then they'd have a good laugh, at her expense. If this happened, her nightmare would be over. It was this faint hope that she clung to as she was jostled roughly down the mountainside.

Lucy was thirstier than she'd ever been before, for the vile rag inside her mouth sopped up every bit of moisture. She ached all over and her stomach felt queasy from the awkward position she'd been forced into. If only she could go back to the previous evening and make a wiser choice, she'd give everything she had. As it was, she was giving up all that she had anyway, including all of the years that she would have lived, otherwise. During the last hour of darkness, Lucy Craddock surrendered to despair.

"Hey, it's them," she heard Gooch say. "Come on, let's get a move on."

They led her horse at a faster pace. The groan that escaped her throat was effectively muffled by the rag in her mouth. But mercifully the motion soon stopped. Large hands dragged her roughly to the ground.

"So you two saddle bums let yourselves be captured

by Wakefield and the old man that's riding with him," accused a voice with an arrogant tone.

Lucy twisted around just enough to see who had spoken. The man was dressed in fancy boots and clothes that were almost new, but he had a coldness in his expression and manner. No doubt, this was Mr. Rumbaugh. He was, indeed, dressing down the former prisoners, but not for mistreating their benefactress. They were in serious trouble for having been caught by their boss's enemies. *The story about that Polish man's ranch being burned and his hired hands being shot was true.*

She realized that since that story was true, then all the rest of it must be true as well. She wondered how she could have been such an arrogant, gullible fool. What must all of those men up at the cave be thinking of her now? She rarely worried about what other people thought of her, or of the things that she did, but this was an exception. She'd really messed up this time. Those two prisoners would lead Rumbaugh and his outlaws right back to that cave, and they'd kill everyone there, including Henry. It was hard to believe that she could feel any worse than she had over the past few hours, but she did.

Rumbaugh came over and jerked Lucy to her feet. Then he squatted, slipped a knife from his belt, and cut the rope that bound her ankles. She stamped her feet a few times, in an effort to bring back some circulation.

"She might be useful to us," he said. "Maybe we can get them two-bit ranchers and Wakefield to surrender without a fight if we display her out there in front of us, and tell them what we'll do to her if they don't."

"Good idea, boss," Gooch said. "They're holed up in a cave way up yonder."

He pointed in the general direction of the hideout.

If Lucy had felt fear before, what she was feeling now was pure terror. Wakefield had been telling the truth, but she'd taken an instant dislike to him, and everything he'd said sounded like lies to her. While the man she'd pinned her hopes on was nothing but a cold-blooded killer. And she couldn't even say that she hadn't been warned.

"First, let's have something to eat before we leave," Darby said. "We're about half starved."

Even Lucy could tell that was the wrong thing to have said when she saw the expression on Rumbaugh's face.

"I spent half the night rounding up horses," he replied in a chilling voice, "and now I intend to get my hands on the ones who're responsible for running 'em off. The rest of us have already eaten, and I don't intend to let you hare-brains hold us up any longer."

Darby knew when to shut up and do what he was told.

"Are you saying that we should just ride up to their hideout?" asked a man who appeared to be second in command.

"Nope. But I expect we could if we made sure to keep that fool woman in plain sight. They're not about to shoot one of their own, especially her."

The part about being one of their own caused Lucy another stab of regret. She'd acted like an adversary, not like one of their own.

Unexpectedly, Rumbaugh took his knife and freed her hands.

"Get on your horse and get ready to ride," he ordered. "If you cause any trouble, at all, you'll live to regret it, but you won't live very long."

Lucy pulled the filthy rag from her mouth and mounted the horse that she'd stolen earlier from the men at the cave.

"Boss, they must have missed her as soon as it got daylight," the second in command said. "They're apt to be on her trail, right now. If it had just been Gooch and Darby, they might have figured it was good riddance, but they'll want Ben Craddock's niece back."

"Probably. But if she'd sneaked around and turned my prisoners loose, and then run off with 'em, I sure wouldn't come after her. I'd say good riddance to her too."

Lucy's spirits sank even lower, for that's what Wakefield's attitude most likely would be. Henry might be able to persuade them to help her, though. Even while she was thinking it, she knew full well that Henry wasn't a persuasive man. But maybe the softer-hearted ones of the group might give in and try to rescue her. She knew it wasn't much to pin her hopes on, for the chances of their survival against Rumbaugh and his men were slim.

"They have any guards posted up there?" Rumbaugh asked.

"One," Darby said. "They always kept one of 'em hid out away from the cave. He could see the approaches."

Rumbaugh grunted like he wasn't surprised at what he heard.

"It should be easy enough to pick off one man," he said.

"What if we run into them coming after the woman?" Courtney asked.

"In that case, it'll save us the trouble of going up there and routing them all out of their hideout. Remember, we've got what they want and they're not going to take the chance of getting a lady hurt."

"Do you think they'll surrender when they've got no guarantee that you'll not kill her anyway? They'll surely know you've got to get rid of all of them—her included."

"Courtney, you worry too much," Rumbaugh said. "They'll assume that I wouldn't do such a thing to a woman."

"I hope you're right, boss."

They started off, and even though Lucy's hands and feet were unbound and she was riding upright in the saddle, there was no chance for her to make a break. She was surrounded by outlaws who didn't trust her for a second. Still, she would keep alert for her chance. She had no intention of dying if she could help it, and what they didn't know was that she'd retrieved her derringer before leaving the cave. It rested in the pocket of her riding skirt. It wasn't much, but if she got the chance to use it, it might make all the difference.

Chapter Ten

Shad stood a little distance apart from the others while they were packing their gear. He was disgusted to think that Lucy Craddock had even considered such a stupid action, let alone carried it out. Even worse, she'd somehow gotten away with it. Before she'd released the prisoners and run off with them to find Rumbaugh, the odds against them had been tough enough. Now, they were downright deplorable. There was now a sense of urgency among the men who chose to ride with him, for it was clear to them that Lucy Craddock had pretty much signed her own death warrant. It was likely that she'd signed theirs, as well.

He couldn't help thinking that Henry Craddock was a sorry sight. The bank clerk kept looking in the direction of the forest as if hoping that his sister would magically reappear. All the while, he alternately sighed and wrung his hands. It was evident to all of them that he didn't have much hope they'd find his sister alive.

Old Ben Craddock's nephew had confided to Abe that he'd been a schoolmaster before becoming a bank clerk. Neither job could have done much to prepare him for what he was having to face now. He didn't know how Craddock would make out in a confrontation with the outlaws, but the man had reached a state of mind where he didn't seem to think he had anything else to lose. That kind of attitude could spawn courage where none had existed before.

Cory was another pitiful-looking fellow. Even after his ribs were bound, and Joe and Abe had doctored the rest of his injured body as much as possible, he was obviously still in pain. Not to mention he was about to embark on his second long ride without rest—his third since the beating he'd taken.

For that matter, Shad didn't figure he looked so good, himself. He ached for even a brief period of uninterrupted sleep. Those few hours he'd gotten the day before were only a vague memory, and every muscle and sinew in his body was exhausted. But there was no help for it. They had to leave the cave, and they had to do it right away.

"Better saddle up," he said.

They moved to follow his order, except for Abe. He approached Shad with a look of concern.

"Son, you're not thinking that we should ride down the mountainside and meet them owlhoots head on?"

"No," he answered. "That's a sure way to get us

killed. I've got another idea. We're going to find a place that we can defend, one where they won't be expecting us. Then the rest of you will wait there for Rumbaugh. He'll come after us. He has to. While you're waiting, I'm going to ride on ahead and scout them out. If I can, I'll get the Craddock woman away from them, if she's still alive. If I can't, I'll try to worry 'em as much as possible."

"Looks to me like you've given yourself the best job," Abe said. "What do you say to my going with you?"

Shad shook his head.

"No, not this time. I appreciate the offer, but you'd better stay with the others. They're going to need you. And don't let Mc Nary follow me like he did before, either."

Abe looked sheepish, confirming Shad's suspicion that he'd known about, and approved of, Mc Nary's night ride.

"Shadrach, you're just like your pa always used to be. That man wouldn't back down from nothin'. He never stopped to consider whether or not the odds were against him. He just went ahead regardless, and all but that one time, he came through, somehow."

It gave Shad a good feeling to be compared to his father. He knew that he didn't deserve the comparison, but it pleased him anyway.

"Where do you think we can find this other place that we can defend?" Abe asked. "Have you got any ideas?"

The truth was that Shad was running out of ideas. He had only one.

"I noticed some boulders overlooking the trail on our way up here. They'd provide us with cover, and at the same time, they'd give us a good view of everything below."

"Well, I just hope that we can get to the place before we run into Rumbaugh's outfit. They're sure to be coming up here, once they get hold of them two prisoners who can tell them right where to go."

Shad figured they had a good chance, and it was their only chance.

By this time, the others were ready to go. They'd overheard what he said about the boulders.

"Do any of you have a better idea?" Shad asked. "If so, now's the time to speak up."

"Your plan sounds good to me," Mc Nary agreed. "I sure can't come up with a better one."

It turned out that the others felt the same way, so they moved out through the pines and scrub and headed down the mountain.

The day was a dark one. Clouds were gathering around the peaks above them. Later on, it would surely rain. Shad dreaded the dangerous lightning that was drawn to mountaintops, along with the flooding and the slippery mud that would result from a storm. This was yet another reason for them to hurry and get themselves to safer place.

He thought of the Judge and wondered how he would have handled the challenge of Rumbaugh and his gang, had he been in Trinidad that day he was needed. Maybe this could all have been avoided, somehow. But he had to concede that the Judge couldn't have done much. It was immediate action that was required, and the time to wait around was a luxury that Shad couldn't afford.

More than an hour passed before they finally made their way down to the boulders. The massive hunks of granite obviously weighed many tons. There were three of them perched delicately on the mountainside as if a giant hand had stopped them in their downward plunge. Shad led the others to the new hideout, and there they took their positions behind the stone fortress. There they would wait. Above them, an ominous rumbling warned of the coming storm. As soon as they'd settled in, Shad took his leave of them and headed on down the mountainside alone.

"Godspeed," he heard Henry Craddock whisper as he went by.

Shad took off away from the trail and rode roughly parallel to it. All the while, he kept himself hidden as he worked his way down toward the place where the outlaws had made their camp. A fork of lightning streaked across the dark sky. The clap of thunder that quickly followed startled the sorrel.

"Easy, boy, easy," he soothed as he brought his mount under control.

He stopped then, and took his slicker from one of the saddlebags. He managed to don it just in time for the deluge. Water streamed around the edges of his hat and over his slicker-protected shoulders, surrounding him with a thick curtain of rain.

The sorrel was nervous, and with good reason. Lightning repeatedly lashed out on and around the peaks, putting on a show that was both fascinating and terrifying. Nature was displaying her power with gusto. He wondered how the men were faring back at the boulders, and figured they were probably doing at least as well as himself.

With his head down, he rode slowly and carefully among the pines. He had no idea about when or where the outlaws had regrouped, although he expected they'd manage to round up most of their horses and do just that. The fact of the matter was, he was riding blind, straight into the unknown.

All the while he was working his way downward, he stayed close to the trail that he'd taken on the journey up the mountain the day before. It was his guess that the former prisoners would lead their outfit up that same trail. Unless he was mistaken about this, the new hideout was perfectly situated for Abe, Kaminski, and the others to intercept them.

He thought about the Craddock woman. Was there a reason for Rumbaugh to let her live for awhile? He could think of only one: shove her out in front of them, where her brother and the rest of the men could see her, and it would effectively shut down a gun battle. Rumbaugh would have to know how strong a leverage she would be for bringing about a surrender. However, Shad didn't see it quite that way. He knew that surrender would mean certain death for Lucy Craddock, anyway. It would mean death, as well, for the men who laid their weapons down to save her. His friends would be aware of this too.

Strangely, Shad's thoughts drifted to another woman, one that he'd never see again. He could think of Letitia without pain, now, and he did so from time to time. As he remembered all the things he'd admired about her, he found himself comparing Letitia with Lucy. If you considered only their beauty, they were about equal. In other ways, though, they weren't equal at all. He knew Lucy's kind. She was a predator, like one of the big cats. She was out to get what she wanted no matter who it hurt, no matter who she had to take it away from. There was a core of toughness in her that refused to give way to feminine softness and sentiment. Not to mention that she was a manipulator, willing to do anything to get her own way. The concept of loyalty was alien to her, the same as it was alien to Luke Crane. It seemed to him that it was the Luke Cranes and the Lucy Craddocks of the world that made it possible for outlaws like Rumbaugh to run roughshod over decent folks. Still, he hoped she was alive. Her character flaws, no matter how severe, didn't merit a death sentence. Unfortunately, Rumbaugh was a woman killer.

The storm that drenched the mountainside was typical for the Southwest. The sky seemed to open up and dump great vats of water onto the Earth. Then, as suddenly as it had started, the rain stopped. Shad drew a deep breath of moist, sweet air. Everything around him was fresh and verdant. Droplets fell from branches, making it appear that the pines were dripping jewels.

Shad took his hat and dumped the water from its brim, shaking it for good measure. Two chipmunks scampered across the ground in front of him, having emerged from their storm shelter. The outlaws would be on the move again, too.

Shad was concealed in the denseness of the forest when he heard the sound of voices and horses on the move. Quickly, he took off his slicker and packed it away so it wouldn't be spotted. Then he rode forward to see if he could catch a glimpse of the riders. He caught sight of them below, and counted fifteen men and one woman.

They were beginning a climb up a curving slope that was steep and rain-slick. It was slow going and sometimes treacherous, for it was hard in places for the horses to get a purchase. He was relieved to see that the woman was with them. That she was still alive made it obvious that Rumbaugh believed she could still be useful to him. She was riding almost midway in the column, and there was no doubt that she was a prisoner. Her hair hung down around her shoulders in wet strands, and her head drooped in weariness, or perhaps in despair. Every shred of arrogance had disappeared. Shad figured she could expect to live as long as it took them to get to the boulders. At that point, she would either be shot because Abe and the others refused to surrender, or else because they did surrender and she was no longer needed. Her only hope for survival was if Shad could manage to get her away from them before the showdown.

He drew the Winchester from its scabbard and put

the lead man in his sights. Then he adjusted his aim slightly forward and fired. There was a dull splat, causing a fountain of mud to spray upward. The startled horse whinnied in fright and reared. Its rider was nearly thrown as he fought to regain control. The others halted and looked around trying to catch a glimpse of the sniper. To a man, they had their pistols out ready to kill him. One of them fired off a shot in Shad's general direction, but it was way off the mark.

Quiet as a ghost, he moved around so he could attack from a different angle. When the column started climbing again, he repeated his performance. Order turned into a mass of confusion. None of them wanted to die that day. In their hurry to get out of harm's way, they'd forgotten all about the woman. Lucy Craddock's head was up now, and she was looking around for a familiar face.

"Get out of the way, all of you," Rumbaugh yelled, "or I'm riding straight over your backsides."

Shad stood there watching the mad scramble for safety, noting that none of Rumbaugh's men were paying the slightest bit of attention to the man who was paying them top dollar to carry out his orders.

Lucy Craddock had the presence of mind to get out of their way. Once she was no longer surrounded, she kicked her big gray horse in the sides and went in the opposite direction from the outlaws. She rode straight up the slope toward the place where Shad was waiting.

Chapter Eleven

Rumbaugh had lost control of his men. They had no military discipline, and it was every man for himself when bullets started flying from the wooded ridge above them. Rumbaugh was furious at their disarray, and berating them for their failure to obey his orders. But the major part of his attention was still on getting himself to safety. Lucy Craddock had been forgotten, and she was making the best of it.

Shad watched helplessly as her mount struggled to stay upright on the slick mud surface. Once, he feared the big gray was going down, but it was game. It stayed on its feet and drove hard for the top.

Come on, he willed the horse. *Faster. You can do it.*

From where he was positioned, he could see that Lucy Craddock's face was a mask of fierce determination. It was clear that she desperately wanted to live and was grabbing the only chance she had. She'd found out the hard way that her esteemed Mr. Rumbaugh was an outlaw and a killer, just like they'd all told her. This was evident in the way she kicked the sides of the gray, urging it to greater speed. She had to be aware that a bullet from an outlaw's gun could cut her down at any moment. Shad was aware of this, too. He kept a sharp look-out.

Suddenly, out of the corner of his eye, he caught the glint of reflected light on a metal gun barrel. Lucy Craddock's life was in the balance. The outlaw holding the weapon was crouched behind some low-lying scrub, down where the trail first began to climb sharply. His gun was aimed at the fleeing woman. Shad figured that it took a real piece of scum to shoot a woman in the back, but Rumbaugh was scum and he'd hired even more of it.

There was no time to take careful aim. He threw his rifle to his shoulder and squeezed off a shot. There was an outcry as the bullet hit its mark. This brought a torrent of gunfire in response, but he'd already moved away. The big gray was close to the top, now. Shad laid down three quick shots in succession to keep the outlaws too worried about their own hides to trouble themselves with hers.

When the horse reached the top, Lucy Craddock didn't stop to seek out her defender, but headed straight for cover. Shad fired one last shot before he turned and followed her.

The forest was thick here, and she was heading off

course into the unknown. It took her a moment to realize this. When she did, she reined up. He rode up beside her.

She looked across at him and recognized him with a start. Dirt streaked her face, and her auburn hair was no longer coifed as it had been before her defection to the outlaws. Instead, it hung limply in wet tangles. All in all, Lucy Craddock was a bedraggled sight. Her arrogance was gone, and the smell of fear was on her.

"Thank you for what you did," she managed to say, but he noticed that the words seemed to come out hard.

"No trouble at all," he responded with sarcasm.

It wasn't lost on her.

"Look, I'm sorry I didn't believe you. I was stupid. If it's any consolation, I paid a high price for that stupidity. Now that I'm free, I'm going to do whatever it takes to avenge my uncle's death."

It was a pretty speech, but he suspected that she was a whole lot more interested in avenging the things Rumbaugh had done to her personally. Not the least of which, was making her look foolish.

"Come on," he said. "We've got to get away from here or you won't be free for long. You'll be dead."

"Where are we going? Back to the cave? Those outlaws know all about the cave from what Darby and Gooch have told them."

And all the thanks for that goes to you, Miss Craddock, he thought.

"I'm sure they do," he said simply. "Come along with me, or stay behind. It's entirely up to you."

She glared at him.

"Fine," she said, "but I need a drink of water first. That vile outlaw stuffed a filthy rag in my mouth."

He handed her the canteen and watched her take a couple of gulps of water. Then she handed it back.

"Let's go," he ordered.

They rode as fast as the dense growth would allow, as they penetrated deeper into the forest that covered the mountainside.

"Where's my brother?" she asked, after a time. "He's not still hiding up there at that cave, is he?"

"No, he left with the others. He's safe—for now."

He could tell that the woman still didn't trust him, not even after what he'd done for her. She was the kind who wanted to do things her own way, and she insisted on always being right. She intimidated others by the force of her will, but this time intimidation wasn't working. It hadn't worked with the outlaws, and it wasn't working with him.

He imagined poor Henry must have had a difficult life trying to appease a sister who was always telling him what to do and what to think. *Well, Lucy Craddock is her brother's problem. At least she is, once I get her safely back to him.*

"I'm soaked all the way to the bone and I'm freezing," she complained loudly.

He knew this was true, for she'd been given no protection from the rain. However, they didn't have much of a lead. They couldn't afford to stop.

"Those outlaws won't wait long before they figure out they can climb that slope without being shot at.

As soon as they do, they're going to be coming after us."

"I know, but I think I'm going to turn to ice."

Now that the excitement of her escape had worn off, her teeth were chattering so hard that he could scarcely make out what she was saying. He reached back for a wool blanket and tossed it over to her.

"Here. Cover up with this. It's the best I can do for now."

He noted that it was a lot more than the outlaws had done for her.

She draped it over her head and around her shoulders. The blanket provided enough warmth to silence her complaints.

Behind him, in the distance, he heard one of Rumbaugh's men shout. It seemed he'd found their trail.

"Come on," Shad urged. "They're getting closer."

He saw her looking back with apprehension.

Shad's need for sleep had long since evaporated, and every nerve in his body was alert. He was heading up the mountain in the general direction of the boulders now. Without the girl, Rumbaugh had lost an ace from the hand he was playing, and Shad and his friends had gained one. But the two of them were in a race with Rumbaugh and his men. It was a race that they had to win.

"Come on, boys, it looks like they went this way," one of the outlaws called.

Shad didn't have a lot of choices. He couldn't send Lucy on ahead while he fought a holding action, for she'd never be able to find her way through the wilderness to the new hideout. He had to keep her with him.

"Keep going!" he said.

As she did, he dropped behind a little and drew his rifle out of the scabbard. With one swift movement, he swung around and fired in the direction of the voice. He didn't have any expectation that the bullet would hit a human target, but at least it would let them know that he was still fighting back. It would also serve to remind them that following him and Lucy Craddock was a dangerous choice. Possibly this might slow them down and make them more cautious. If so, his chances of making it to the fortress of boulders with their former hostage would be much improved.

"Watch it!" someone yelled. "He's shooting again."

"It's got to be Wakefield. Don't let him get away!"

Shad recognized Rumbaugh's voice. He urged his mount forward and caught up with Lucy Craddock.

It was easy to get lost in the vast wilderness of the mountain. It was especially easy when you didn't have a trail to follow. But he knew roughly which way to go, and it was uphill all the way.

The color of the blanket that covered Lucy was a drab green, which blended well with the forest. His own shirt was green wool, and he was thankful that he didn't happen to have on his red one. The harder they were to spot, the better their chances.

They were managing to keep ahead of the outlaws when, without warning, the big gray reared. Shad saw at once the reason for the horse's fright. A large snake was slithering out of the underbrush and across its path. Lucy screamed and struggled for control, but it was to no avail. Before Shad could grab the reins, the big horse bolted, with Lucy hanging on for all she was worth. He raced after her on the sorrel, but the way was difficult. Branches scratched and tore at his sleeves, and even worse, they raked against his face. He could see that Lucy was getting the same kind of rough treatment. The outlaws were sure to have heard her scream, and they'd know something had happened.

It seemed like an eternity before he was able to catch up with the runaway and bring the headlong dash to a halt. Lucy was breathless and her hands were shaking.

"What happened?" she asked.

"A snake spooked him."

"I didn't even see it. I don't suppose this is the way you'd planned to go."

She was right about that. They'd veered far to the south and any hope he'd had of reaching the boulders had vanished. All they could do now was to keep going and try to stay ahead of the enemy. But he knew that the horses would soon tire, and eventually they'd run them to death. He had to admit that their prospects looked bleak.

Another piece of his father's advice came to mind. He'd given it when Shad was a ten-year-old contestant in a foot race that was dominated by boys who were older.

"Son, don't ever give up, even when things look hopeless—especially when things look hopeless. You can't know what Providence, or plain dumb luck, will offer you after the next eye-blink."

At the time, he'd felt the advice was inappropriate. He doubted if Providence or dumb luck, either one, would offer him any help in that foot race. It turned out that he was right, since he'd come in dead last. Later, he understood that his father had simply taken that opportunity to share his philosophy. But right now he desperately needed some good luck or else a whole lot of Divine intervention.

Suddenly, he heard two shots fired in rapid succession. They sounded fairly close, so it was possible they were firing at the snake. Most likely the reptile hadn't taken the precaution of keeping out of their way. Unless he could shake Rumbaugh's men, which now didn't seem likely, his and Lucy's chances of survival ranged from pitiful to none at all. If things could look more hopeless, he didn't know how that could be.

"Come on," he ordered. "We can't just sit here."

"They're going to kill us," she gasped.

"They're shooting wild. They just want to worry us a little."

"What are we going to do?"

He needed to calm her down and give her some hope.

"We're going to keep going uphill and then try to cut back until we can see three big boulders sitting above the trail."

"I know the place," she said. "I remember seeing it on the way to the cave. Is that where Henry and the others are waiting?"

"Yeah. If anything happens to me, you have to try to get there."

He wished, now, that he hadn't ordered Abe to keep Mc Nary with the rest of them. Having Mc Nary along would improve their odds of survival. Maybe not enough, but another gun would help a lot. When you got right down to it, though, he could use the entire outfit.

Chapter Twelve

Rumbaugh was furious as he fought his way back down the slope to safety. He didn't like being shot at, he was surrounded by incompetents, and he cursed the mud that hindered him.

"Stop her!" he yelled, but none of his men seemed interested in following his order since they were all too busy running for cover.

He figured the sniper was one of Wakefield's bunch. Most likely it was Wakefield himself who was causing so much trouble. First the horses were stampeded and the Beale kid was snatched away. Now this.

As soon as he got to a place of safety, he looked back. To his dismay, the Craddock woman was getting away.

He looked around and saw that his men's response was half-hearted at best. He spotted Gooch off to the side, hidden behind some scrub. The man with the squeaky voice raised up a little and aimed his rifle. But he was hit by one of the sniper's bullets before he could get off a shot. He cried out as fell, dropping his rifle into the scrub. Rumbaugh caught a glimpse of the shooter. He guessed it was Wakefield. All around him, his men were repaying their attacker with a barrage of gunfire now. It was if they were trying to redeem themselves.

Rumbaugh's horse shied when another shot from the ridge ricocheted and barely missed hitting the animal. His cover wasn't as good as he'd thought. He moved farther back into the trees.

As much as it irked him to let Wakefield and old Ben Craddock's niece get away, that slick, dangerous trail up the side of the mountain was a big obstacle. It was even a deathtrap when it was peppered with lead.

"Hold your fire!" he ordered his men.

The silence that followed was almost ghostly after the din of the gun battle.

"Do you think he's still up there?" Courtney asked after a moment.

"We'll wait a little longer and see."

The moments dragged by, and during that time Rumbaugh's anger seethed. At last, he could stand it no longer.

"Come on, let's go after him," he commanded his men. "I want Wakefield and that Craddock woman, and I'll pay the man who kills them a hundred and fifty dollars extra for each one of 'em."

Three hundred dollars was a lot of money, but he'd learned long ago that if you wanted something, you paid for it. He wanted Wakefield and the woman bad, and the bigger the reward you offered, the quicker the results.

One thing troubled him, though. Wakefield appeared to have been alone and he knew there were others. He wondered where they were holed up, and why they weren't with him. He didn't discount the possibility of an ambush. Counting the Beale kid, he figured there must be about ten of 'em. They were sure to have abandoned that cave once they discovered that Darby and Gooch had escaped with word of its whereabouts. When he considered the caliber of his own sorry outfit, he admitted that ten disgruntled ranchers could cause him a lot of trouble. He was going to have to take down their leader. If the men he'd hired couldn't do it, he'd have to kill Wakefield himself.

In spite of the reward that he'd just offered, none of his men were rushing to obey his order. To his disgust they were milling around like steers, eyeing the muddy slope as if it were a road to the slaughterhouse. Rumbaugh fought back his disgust and tried again.

"Get a move on! I'm paying every last one of you top dollar, and I intend to get my money's worth."

Courtney was the first to ride out. Rumbaugh watched him glance furtively at the wooded area where the sniper had hidden. His *segundo* was ready to retreat at the first sign of danger. The going was slow, but Courtney made his way upward without incident. Once he was safely at the top, the others followed. Rumbaugh went last.

At the top, they made a quick search of the area. Wakefield and the woman had left.

"Track 'em," Rumbaugh ordered.

Courtney got down on his haunches and looked for tracks.

"They went that way, Boss," he said, pointing to an unmarked stretch of wilderness.

"Then what are you waiting for? Let's go."

Courtney hesitated.

"The rest of their outfit might be back there somewhere. They could ambush us, and Mc Nary is with 'em—he's one of the best shots I've ever seen."

Silently Rumbaugh cursed his former hired hand and Wakefield, too. Fear of them was causing him to lose his hold over his men.

"Do you think that I'm paying the lot of you top wages to do something safe like shovel manure and plant petunias?" he asked. "You're going to do your job, or else I'm going to make sure you regret that you didn't."

With that threat, Rumbaugh headed off in the direction that Courtney had pointed out. He didn't look back, but he could tell the others were following, albeit reluctantly.

Rumbaugh considered his enemy. According to that simpleton Crane who'd hired him, Wakefield tended to be a loner. He could work with others and enjoy their company, but he didn't mind being alone, either.

That fact might work against him. If, true to his nature, he'd pulled off the rescue on his own, it meant that he was separated from his men. Alone, he'd be easy to take care of. That meant the woman would be easy to dispose of, as well.

In spite of the possible danger, Rumbaugh couldn't be more eager. He sensed that he was very close to securing everything he'd always wanted. He had only to get rid of Wakefield, the woman, and the men who rode with them. His reward would be a huge chunk of land, herds of cattle, vast wealth, and best of all, formidable power in the halls of the Territorial Congress.

He wished his old man could see him now. Carlton Rumbaugh could jolly well choke on his contempt. He'd have to take back all of his putdowns and all of the insults that he'd been so generous with. The fact was that he'd become a bigger, better man than Carlton Rumbaugh ever dreamed of being. The thought gave him a lot of satisfaction and reinforced his determination. There was far too much at stake to let a saddle bum like Wakefield, and the ones who'd sided with him, jeopardize his future.

Courtney had ridden up and passed him as he followed the trail their quarry had left.

"Come on! They went this way!" his foreman called.

This was followed by a rifle shot.

"Watch it, he's shooting at us again," Darby warned.

Rumbaugh's heartbeat quickened with excitement.

He was close. Back when he was a boy, his father used to take him hunting at night with coon hounds, and he'd always felt this same way whenever those hounds treed one of the bright-eyed nocturnal animals.

"Don't you dare let Wakefield and that woman get away," he warned. "If you do I'll make you regret it."

The truth was, he was having a tough time following them, himself. Needled branches smacked him in the face and tore at his clothes. Also, he had to be constantly alert. But the necessity of killing Wakefield and that troublesome female drove him on.

Suddenly he heard the sound of a frightened horse. It was followed immediately by a woman's scream.

"Up there," said Courtney, pointing in the direction where the sounds had come. "We've got 'em now."

Rumbaugh strained his eyes in order to catch a glimpse of them, but the trees were too thick and his view was blocked.

"Come on, let's put an end to this," he ordered, unable to keep the excitement from his voice.

They plunged headlong through the narrow spaces, ignoring the scratches they were getting, and the pounding from limbs. But by the time they reached the place, both the woman and Wakefield were gone.

Courtney reined up and the others followed suit.

"Over there," he pointed at the half-hidden reptile. "It's a snake. That must have been what all the ruckus was about."

Rumbaugh hated snakes, even though this one had done him a favor.

"Shoot it," he ordered.

Courtney pulled out his revolver and fired a couple of shots into the offending creature.

"Wakefield and the Craddock woman took off in that direction," said Courtney when he'd finished. "It's strange too. That wasn't the way they were headed before. I guess they know what they're doing, but it sure don't make much sense to me."

"The snake probably startled the horse," Darby observed. "It might have bolted and the other horse took out after it."

His theory sounded plausible to Rumbaugh. If the runaway horse had taken them in a different direction from their allies, so much the better. There wasn't much they could do. Rumbaugh was feeling pretty good now, in spite of the danger and the discomfort from his scratches and bruises. It was only a little matter of time before his future was secure.

Chapter Thirteen

It was clear to Shad that they couldn't go on much longer. The horses were tiring. To survive, they had to find a place where they could make a stand. His best hope was that Abe and the others would hear the gunfire and find them in time to make a difference. Other than that, all he could expect to do was hold out as long as possible against superior numbers.

Suddenly, their limited possibilities grew even more limited. Ahead of them rose a stone outcropping, effectively blocking their escape. If they turned to the side, they'd have to go more deeply into the wilderness where they'd be run down by Rumbaugh and his gang. The only chance they had was to climb. They had to do it quickly, though, for they couldn't let themselves get caught by the outlaws while they were clinging to the face of that rock. He spotted a narrow ledge that might hide them if they could reach it in time.

"Follow me," he called to Lucy, "and do exactly as I say."

When they reached the outcropping, he stopped at the base and dismounted. Lucy reined up beside him.

"Oh, no," she wailed. "We're trapped and they're going to kill us."

"Maybe. Maybe not. Dismount."

"What?"

"Look, there's no time to argue. Get down off that horse."

She climbed down, all the while looking at him like he'd taken leave of his senses. He grabbed the canteen. His pistol was already strapped to his side.

Lucy had pinned the blanket around her like a cape, so he didn't expect that it would inhibit her climb. But she turned to him with a look of concern.

"We're going up that rock wall," he said.

"You're crazy! What about the horses? We can't just leave them here."

In answer, he gave the sorrel a sharp slap on the rump. "Go!" he said. The sorrel took off like a shot. The gray was close behind it.

That didn't set well with Lucy Craddock.

"Now, you've gone and stranded us," she said, her expression one of disbelief.

"Come on!" he ordered.

He slipped his arm through the canteen strap and climbed. Up close, the wall of stone was far from smooth as it appeared at a distance. Thanks to the work of wind and water, it had chinks and eroded spots that could be used for footholds and handholds. Cliff-climbing wasn't something he would have chosen, but this was the only way they'd have even a ghost of a chance.

Once he glanced back and saw Lucy struggling along behind him. It was just before the easy portion of the climb ended. After that, he had to look for places that would serve as handholds. In the distance, he could hear the outlaws crashing through the wilderness.

The urgency of the situation propelled him upward as he clawed his way over the stone surface. Lucy Craddock's survival instincts appeared to be as great as his own, for she never faltered.

"Hurry," she urged. "They're getting close."

Now he could see the ledge. It was only a few feet above the highest point he could reach. He stretched and grabbed for the next handhold, a mere niche in the surface, and pulled himself up to the narrow shelf. Once there, he reached down and grabbed Lucy Craddock's hand. One great heave and she was beside him, panting to catch her breath. His hands were raw from contact with the rough-surfaced rock, and it looked like hers were in at least as bad a shape as his own.

He pulled her away from the edge, and they both flattened themselves against the back wall.

"Keep still," he whispered.

Her look told him that it had been a foolish order.

Now he could hear Rumbaugh and his men below. They approached the outcropping, where they stopped.

They were so close that he could make out what they were saying.

"They've disappeared, Boss. I don't know how they could have done it. They weren't all that far ahead of us."

The next voice was filled with fury.

"I want to know what happened to 'em! The ground didn't swallow them up and they sure as the dickens can't fly."

Shad dared not risk looking over the ledge, but he heard them milling around looking for sign.

"Well, Boss," said the one that had spoken first. It looks to me like they turned and headed off toward the south. That's the way those horse tracks lead, anyway."

"That sounds logical," the man who had to be Rumbaugh agreed. "They sure wouldn't have turned back, and they couldn't ride up that outcrop. It seems to me that they didn't have any choice but to go south."

"Okay, Boss, let's go get 'em."

Shad realized that he'd been holding his breath. Against the odds, it looked like they were going to make it. Then Rumbaugh spoke.

"Hold on a minute," said the outlaw. "Ames, you stay here just in case them two decide to double back on us."

"Right, Boss. If I shoot 'em do I get the reward?"

"Shoot 'em first, and then we'll talk about your reward."

"If they double back, you've got it made, Ames,"

said one of the other outlaws. "It almost don't seem fair."

It seemed strange to Shad to be lying there listening to others anticipating his death with such pleasure. Then he heard the horses ride off. He knew they didn't have much time, for when Rumbaugh and his men found the sorrel and the gray without riders, they'd hightail it right back to Ames. About all he'd succeeded in doing was to buy himself and Lucy a few extra minutes. Now, he'd have to figure out how to use them. He'd been caught flat-footed without that escape route that his father had warned him to have. But the truth of it was, desperate situations often came without escape routes. They couldn't climb down with the outlaw on guard below, for he'd be all too eager to earn his reward. There was nothing left for them but the ledge.

He touched Lucy's shoulder to get her attention. Then he put his finger to his lips, warning her not to make any noise. She didn't hide her resentment. He ignored her expression and pointed forward. Then he began to inch along the ledge.

For something like the hundredth time, he wished that he hadn't told Abe to keep Mc Nary at the boulders. But what he'd had in mind when he left the fortress was to find the woman, grab her, and run. It had worked in freeing Cory, and he'd figured that it was the only way of getting Lucy away from Rumbaugh.

He crawled farther along the ledge, hoping that it would lead them away from danger. It was impossible to tell how far it went, for the wall of stone curved about a dozen yards beyond, and he couldn't see the end of it. If they could make it around the curve, at least they wouldn't be so easy to spot from below. Once they were out of sight, he figured maybe they could find a way to climb to the top and make their escape.

He risked a glance below, and saw Ames standing beside his horse, building a smoke. His attention was focused on his tobacco sack, at least for the moment.

At last, they both made it safely around the curve without being seen. Shad's sense of relief was short-lived though, for this was only the beginning. He saw that a few yards farther along there was a crevice that led to the top. It was narrow and steep, but it offered a way out.

He made his way closer and looked up. The escape route was only wide enough to accommodate the body of one person at a time, and climbing it would be much like inching his way up a chimney that was three stories high.

He looked back at the woman.

"This is our only way out," he whispered. "Are you game?"

"I don't want to die, Wakefield," she said softly. "Yes, I'm game."

Shad positioned himself inside the narrow crevice and began to work his way upward. Again, he used whatever handholds and footholds he could find, but often he had to resort to wedging his body between the two walls and pushing himself toward the top.

He could hear Lucy struggling with her own climb only a few feet below. She was a difficult woman, and he couldn't find much to admire about her, but when the chips were down, she seemed determined to do whatever it took to save herself.

The rough stone sides tore at the skin of his already sore hands. Wedging himself, he pulled off his bandanna and wrapped it around one of them. Then he took his knife and cut the tail of his shirt to wrap the other.

"How are your hands faring?" he asked Lucy.

"Terrible. I wrapped my handkerchief around one and my scarf around the other. It helps a little. But I hate heights. It makes me sick to think about climbing all way up there."

"Don't think about it," he warned, "and whatever you do, don't look down."

That worn-out piece of advice was all that he had to give her, and he doubted if he was telling her anything that she didn't already know.

With determination born of necessity, he continued the tortuous climb. Foot by foot, he claimed the rock chimney, until he was finally able to pull himself over the top. He caught his breath and reached down to help Lucy. He saw that her hands were a mess, as much of a mess as his own. When she was safely on level ground, she started to tremble. He didn't know if it was from cold or from fear. Probably it was due to both. For a time, they just lay there near the edge, panting and resting from their exertions.

"We're not out of this yet, are we?" Lucy asked when her breathing was back to normal.

"Nope. But we're a lot better off than we were before."

He sincerely hoped that he was telling her the truth.

Chapter Fourteen

While Shad lay beside the exhausted woman, he heard the outlaws return. Although they were far below, he recognized Rumbaugh's voice. He was questioning the guard he'd left behind. Lucy Craddock reached over and touched Shad's shoulder in dismay. He put his finger to his lips for silence while he listened.

"Did you see any sign of Wakefield?" Rumbaugh demanded to know.

"No," came the reply. "I thought you took out after 'em cause they were headed that way."

"That no-account saddle bum fooled us," he said. "Them horses were riderless. Him and that girl must have took off on foot. That means they're hiding around here someplace."

Shad knew that time was running out for them, for

it wouldn't take the outlaws long to figure out what
they'd done. They'd soon find their way to the top of
the outcrop, one way or another. This didn't leave him
a choice. They were going to have to make it to the
boulders on foot. He didn't know if Lucy had the sta-
mina for it, but she did have plenty of determination.
He'd give her that. She was watching him intently, her
eyes wide with fear.

"Let's go," he mouthed.

Keeping low, so as not to be skylined, they made
their way back, away from the drop-off. It was only a
few yards until they reached the cover of the trees.
Again, he had reason to be thankful that Lucy's blanket and his own clothes blended so well with the soft
greens of the wilderness.

"What are we going to do, now?" Lucy asked. "If
they find a way to ride up here, we can't outrun their
horses."

She'd voiced his own concern.

"We're going to have to keep ahead of them and
hide when we have to. Then we'll find our way back
to where your brother and the others are waiting."

"Do you know where that is?"

After the incident with the snake, they'd changed
direction and he had no way of knowing how far
they'd come. Still, he had a good idea that the boulders
lay to the northwest of their present position.

"I can make a good guess," he said.

"Then let's get going. I've had all of Rumbaugh I
can stand."

It seemed that Miss Lucy Craddock's favorable

opinion of the outlaw had changed once she'd met him.

The storm had long since moved out over the plains and the afternoon sun was warming the mountainside, even reaching down between tree branches to dry Lucy Craddock's wet clothing.

Shad had little doubt that there was a way to the top of the outcropping that could be ridden on horseback. He also knew that Rumbaugh's men would look until they found it. It was necessary for him and the woman to keep moving away, for he suspected they didn't have much time.

"If I live through this," Lucy gasped, "I'm going back to Denver and forget all about this awful place."

The thought that came to his mind was *Godspeed and good riddance*. Aloud he said, "I guess that some folks are meant to live in the city."

He glanced over and saw that she was aware of his unspoken sentiment.

They moved deeper into the forest. All around them, the air was heavy with the scent of pine. Beneath their feet lay a thick cushion of pine needles.

"What are the others doing?" she demanded to know. "Are they just sitting up there in a safe place, waiting for us to come riding back?"

She sounded accusatory.

"Yep. We figured that one life was enough to risk getting you away from the outlaws. Besides, we didn't know if you were still alive. The way Rumbaugh felt about you, he was likely to shoot you on sight."

In spite of the fact that she was almost dry and comfortably warm, she shivered.

"None of this was my fault," she argued. "Why should I have believed you? I was told that you were my uncle's killer."

He didn't have any sympathy with her excuses.

"You were also told how and why Rumbaugh murdered your uncle. You were told by others besides myself, and your brother had sense enough to believe the truth."

"My brother is a fool and always has been."

Shad was too tired to argue with her. Besides, he needed to save his breath and put as much distance behind him as possible.

The next time they stopped, it was for water. He offered her the canteen that he'd had the foresight to bring with him.

"Go easy," he warned. "It's all we've got."

She took a couple of swallows and handed it back. He took a drink himself before moving on.

They hadn't gone far when he heard someone calling his name.

"Shadrach!"

Not many would call him that, and certainly no outlaw would. He turned to see Mc Nary riding toward him through the forest. He was alone. It appeared that Mc Nary had slipped away again, or else he'd left the boulders with Abe's tacit permission. Either way, Shad was plenty glad to see him.

"Looks like you've bought yourself some trouble," Mc Nary observed.

Lucy left Shad's side and ran to him, the blanket flying out behind.

"Please, you've got to get me out of here," she begged. "Those outlaws are going to come after me and kill me."

"I expect they're going to try, Ma'am," said Mc Nary. "Looks to me like you need to pick a better class of friends than them two hardcases that you took up with."

Lucy Craddock didn't like being reminded of her foolishness.

"I'll admit that I made a terrible mistake. Now, will you get me out of here! My brother is going to marry an heiress, so I'll be able to pay whatever you ask."

Shad had never much liked the Craddock woman but his dislike suddenly deepened. She was trying to bribe Mc Nary into taking her away on horseback, leaving Shad to face the killers on his own.

"Sorry," Mc Nary said. "I don't hire out to take on passengers."

Lucy Craddock grew bright red in the face and said some words that ladies weren't supposed to say.

Before Mc Nary could answer, there was a shout in the distance.

"Over here! I've spotted their tracks and it looks like they're headed up the mountain."

It had happened, the outlaws had found their way to the top. Shad figured that Mc Nary would have been a lot better off if he'd stayed at the boulders with the others. Still, he was glad to have him and his Colt as allies.

"We sure can't outrun 'em," Mc Nary said, "so it looks like we're going to have to make a stand."

Shad agreed, but they had no cover. He glanced around in desperation for anything that would provide a measure of protection. But there was nothing but an old dead-fall tree. It wasn't much, but it was better than facing the enemy out in the open.

"Over there," he pointed.

They ran for the dead-fall and Lucy Craddock got there first. Mc Nary tied the reins of his buckskin to some nearby brush that would give it a little cover. Then they all hunkered down behind the fallen tree trunk. Shad hoped that its cover would be enough to protect them from their attackers.

"Is there any chance that Abe will miss you and come looking?" Shad asked.

"Abe was with me," he said. "He told me that he didn't want what happened to your father to happen to you. Said he should have been with Dunham when he was shot. Said he wasn't going to make that mistake again. Then when we heard all that gunfire, I came to find you while he went back to fetch the others."

Shad blessed Abe for his loyalty, and he hoped that his old friend could bring help in time.

Just then, he caught a glimpse of one of the outlaws through the trees and heard him call out.

"Hey, they've got a horse and there's three of 'em now!"

"What are you talking about?"

It was the voice of Rumbaugh demanding an answer.

"Wakefield and the woman went that way and somebody on horseback is with them."

Rumbaugh evidently didn't like what he was hearing for he uttered a curse.

"Well, I guess one more won't make much difference," he said. "Let's get a move on. This time they're not going to get away."

If the outlaws kept on the way they were going, they'd ride right over the fallen tree trunk. Shad's .44 was aimed at the nearest rider. Mc Nary was ready, too, with his own revolver. It was then that one of Rumbaugh's men spotted them.

"Over there!" he yelled. "They're behind that log."

Rumbaugh and his men slid from their horses and scattered, taking cover behind trees and scrub. Shad was aware that the odds of his survival were slim to none. Any hope that he'd had of Abe getting back with the others in time to help had just died.

He caught sight of one of the outlaws that they'd captured at Kaminski's burned-out ranch. Then he heard Rumbaugh.

"Wakefield! I know you're over there. Why don't you and that woman, and whoever else is with you, put your guns down and surrender. Make it easy on all of us."

Shad eased up to a firing position. He had the arsonist in his sights.

"All right," said Rumbaugh. "I guess we'll have to do this the hard way."

On his order, the outlaws started firing. The peace of the wilderness was instantly destroyed as bullets hit the fallen tree, sending wood splinters flying.

Shad fired his first shot and watched his former prisoner go down. Beside him, Mc Nary was pouring it on them, as well.

Mc Nary had his rifle as well as a Colt .45. Shad had abandoned his Winchester when he sent the horses on without riders. He was thankful that his partner was there to hold them off while he reloaded. Had he been alone, he wouldn't have stood a chance. They'd have rushed him as soon as he'd emptied the chambers.

The air was thick with gun smoke, and after that first outlaw was hit, it was impossible to tell how much damage they were doing. Targets were hard to spot, and Shad was firing at the last flash of gunfire.

After a time, it appeared that the enemy was moving back. The firing eased off, as well. He guessed that the outlaws had met with more resistance than they'd expected. Together, he and Mc Nary had stopped their assault. Still, he figured the worst was yet to come.

He recalled the attack outside of Trinidad. One of the outlaws had circled around in order to shoot them from behind. He didn't discount the possibility of Rumbaugh using that same tactic again.

He felt a burning sensation on his earlobe. When he touched it, his fingers came away with blood. He figured that a flying splinter must have grazed him, and in the heat of battle, he hadn't noticed.

Mc Nary was using the lull in fighting to reload his weapons. Lucy Craddock had her back to the fallen tree trunk. Her knees were pulled up to her chest and her head was lowered as if to meet them. She was a sorry sight, but at least she wasn't giving them any trouble.

"What do you suppose they're up to?" Mc Nary asked.

"They're pausing before the next round, I expect. We'll soon find out."

They didn't have to wait long before the outlaws started firing again. It wasn't a barrage, as before. This time the shots were sporadic, just enough to keep them pinned down—or distracted. Most of the earlier smoke had cleared and Shad spotted what he'd been watching out for. One of the outlaws was circling around to get behind them. Shad fired a shot at him, but the outlaw was keeping low and moving fast.

Now the others were moving up again. He could see a couple of them crawling forward in the grass, while the ones behind laid down a barrage of cover fire. He'd lost sight of the man who was circling around to their back. Mc Nary needed all the help he could get in order to hold off the frontal attack. Still, Shad had to stop the man who'd set out to back-shoot them. He turned and saw, not one, but two outlaws with their guns drawn. In one swift motion, he brought up the .44 and fired at the nearest of the two. They'd been counting on surprise and that advantage was lost. The outlaw fell but not before he got off a shot. Shad heard the buzz as the bullet passed close to his injured ear. He fired at the other outlaw but heard his gun click on empty. He'd run out of ammunition at the worst possible time. Fully expecting to die, he was surprised when the gun dropped from the outlaw's hand and the big man toppled. He couldn't understand what had happened. Then he saw Lucy. She'd come out of her rolled-up position and was clutching a little lady's pistol in her hand. At close range, a derringer could be as deadly as a Colt. She'd proved this once again. Lucy Craddock had settled at least some of her score with her would-be killers.

"Keep an eye on 'em," he told her as he turned back to reload and help Mc Nary. He was aware that dead men sometimes weren't as dead as they looked.

All of a sudden, he became aware of a more intense level of gunfire. Most of it was coming from off to the side. It appeared that his old friend had arrived.

"Abe," he said to himself. "I owe you one, *amigo*."

Now the outlaws were outnumbered and they knew it. Still, they fought on. Shad heard a cry as one of Abe's men took a hit. But he couldn't see which one it was through the denseness of the growth and the thickness of the smoke. As best he could tell, Abe and the others were moving to surround Rumbaugh's men. More shots were exchanged before the outlaws were forced to surrender.

"You all right, son?" Abe asked as Shad and Mc Nary left their shelter.

"We're fine," he said. "The woman is still back there. Guess she'll come out when she takes a notion."

Abe glanced in the direction of the dead-fall tree. "Guess she will," he said.

"Did we lose any of our men?" asked Shad, remembering the cry he'd heard during the gun battle.

Abe's expression turned grim.
"Afraid so. Slim took a bullet and so did Joe. They didn't make it."

Shad felt an intense sadness, for they were both good men. Cletus would sorely miss his brother, and Cory Beale would have to take on the responsibility of running Joe's ranch by himself.

"I'm sorry about that," he said. "I'd sure like to get my hands on Rumbaugh, but I don't see him anywhere."

"It looks like the big fish got away," said Abe. "He must have slipped off and hid when he saw how things were going."

Shad was uneasy about that. Until he was captured or dead, Rumbaugh was sure to make more trouble.

"We'd better post a guard," he said.

He noticed that Henry Craddock had coaxed his sister from behind the log and was having an affectionate reunion. It looked to Shad like Henry had a lot more regard for his sister than she had for him. It appeared that what Lucy liked about Henry was his fiancée's fortune and social standing.

Abe gave some of the prisoners the task of digging graves. Then they buried the dead outlaws as well as their own fallen men. Cory Beale was taking the death of his uncle hard.

Shad went over to him and offered his condolences.

"Uncle Joe raised me," he said. "I don't know how I'll get along without him."

"You'll do fine. Just be the sensible hard-working man that your uncle taught you to be."

He felt bad about their losses, but freedom had its price, and freedom from the likes of Jake Rumbaugh was what they'd been fighting for.

After the burying was done and they were getting ready to leave, he steeled himself and spoke to Lucy Craddock.

Her clothes were the worse for wear, but she'd pulled her hair back and fixed it into some kind of knot. He could tell by her manner that she was pretty much back to her old self.

"I appreciate what you did with that derringer," he said.

If she could look any haughtier, he couldn't imagine it.

"I didn't shoot that outlaw for your sake," she informed him. "I did it for my own. Anyway, you saved my life once and now I believe that we're even. I've paid my debt."

"Agreed," he replied. Then he turned and walked away. He wished Henry Craddock a whole lot of luck. With a sister like that, he'd need it.

On their way down the mountain, darkness caught up with them, forcing them to spend another night in the wilderness. They posted men to guard the prisoners and to watch for Rumbaugh who was out there someplace, no doubt waiting to make trouble.

Just before Shad fell asleep, he thought about Rumbaugh and about Crane and his men. He wondered if Crane was still looking for him. He couldn't forget how his former boss had been so eager to lynch him, and how his former friends had been willing to hunt him down and put his head in a noose. He had unfinished business with Crane, and he wouldn't be able to walk away from it. He had to face the man and have it out with him.

Chapter Fifteen

Pink ribbons of dawn colored the eastern sky when Shad opened his eyes. A night's rest had made a big difference. In spite of his injured hands and the cut on his ear, he felt renewed and thankful to be alive. He saw that Cletus and Cory were both awake and standing guard over the prisoners. He felt sympathy for them. Cletus's brother and Cory's uncle had both been good men. It would be hard for Cory to run the ranch alone, and even harder for Cletus to manage without the brother he'd depended on. Still, he was confident they'd each find a way to go on alone.

Tied up nearby were the eight outlaws they'd captured. Five members of the gang had been killed. Only Rumbaugh had escaped.

The others were waking up and busying themselves

with different tasks, so Shad crawled out of his bedroll and pulled on his boots.

"You're lookin' a lot better," Abe observed as he handed Shad a cup of freshly-made coffee. Shad figured it must have been the aroma of the hot brew that woke him.

"Thanks," he said, "for the coffee, not the compliment."

Before they rode out, they ate breakfast, and he was glad to be eating full-fledged meals again on what he hoped was becoming a regular basis.

His sorrel and the gray had been recovered, but today he was riding the dun.

As they headed down the mountain with the outlaws in tow, he noticed that Lucy Craddock was sticking close to her brother. They were both staying as far away from Shad as they could get. That was fine with him. He'd had enough of Lucy to last a lifetime.

It was promising to be a far different kind of day than the one before, when the sky had opened up and poured buckets, and lightning had put on a show. Too much blood had been spilled, as well. What they'd been through was harrowing, and he suspected that none of them would ever be the same.

When they neared the base of the mountain, there was a place where he could look out over the plains. Below them was a sobering sight. Luke Crane and the hands from the Circle C had trailed him to the mountain. They'd evidently spotted him and his allies returning with the prisoners, for they were spread out in a line, waiting. He needn't have worried about seeking out his unfinished business, for it had come to him.

"I reckon we've got trouble, son," Abe said. "They must've tracked us, or else they followed Rumbaugh and his outfit."

"Don't worry about it, *amigo*. It's trouble that I'd have gone looking for if it hadn't come looking for me."

"Then I reckon that we'd best go down there and meet it together."

Shad and his allies rode out onto the plain, while Crane and his outfit sat astride their mounts and watched. In front of Crane's line of men, they formed their own line, with the prisoners bunched at one end. The two opposing sides were separated by a short distance of several yards.

When they came to a stop, Crane rode out in front of his line a few paces. He was a big man, with wide shoulders and ham fists. His narrow-set eyes made his beak nose look even more prominent. No one would ever accuse Luke Crane of being a handsome man, especially since his face had such a hard look about it. Not too many would accuse him of being smart, either.

"We're here to hang Wakefield," he announced. "Hand him over."

Abe was the one who spoke up.

"Just who in Colorado Territory are you to be hanging anybody, Crane? You've got no authority to do such a thing. Every man has a right to a trial."

Crane wasn't accustomed to being challenged and he didn't like it.

"I aim to see that justice is done. No trial is needed. That saddle bum used to work for me and he killed two good men."

Abe appeared to be hanging on to this temper with great difficulty.

"Jake Rumbaugh killed both of those men, and a lot more besides. They want him back East to hang him for murder. He wanted the Craddock ranch and he killed its owner to get it. He killed Charlie when he witnessed the murder. Then he tried to kill Miss Craddock and her brother so they wouldn't inherit the ranch that he was trying to grab. Shad Wakefield was the one who saved their lives."

"Where is Jake?" Crane asked, looking around for Rumbaugh. "I'll bet you don't have the nerve to tell those lies in front of him."

Lucy Craddock rode out in front of the line then, big as you please, where she looked Crane square in the eye.

"Rumbaugh is a vicious murderer. He tried to kill me and he almost succeeded. Unfortunately he escaped."

Shad and the others watched as Luke Crane became more and more uncomfortable. He could scarcely call a well-bred city lady like Lucy Craddock a liar. He hadn't anticipated this kind of defense, at all. He'd wanted to find Shad alone and helpless, for he'd already tried him in his own mind, and there was nothing left but to carry out the execution. Now he was being confronted with witnesses to Shad's innocence, and nine of them were armed and ready to defend him to the death. For a tense moment no one moved.

Then Tex left Crane's lineup and rode over to the other side. He turned his horse and faced his boss.

"I told you Shad was innocent," he said in a loud clear voice that everyone could hear, "and you wouldn't even listen to the facts. You wanted your necktie party so bad that it didn't matter you'd be hanging an innocent man. You're just as bad as Jake Rumbaugh."

Before Crane could find his voice to answer, another of his men rode over to join Tex. It was Grimes. He didn't say a word, letting his action say it all. At the start, the numbers had been ten to nine in Crane's favor. But now the odds had changed.

"So that's the way it's going to be, is it!" shouted the enraged rancher.

"Look Crane, you're in the wrong and you're too proud to admit it," Mc Nary said. "You tried to hang an innocent man just to satisfy your blood lust. Why don't you turn around and go on back home."

During Mc Nary's brief speech, another of Crane's men defected, and he was joined by the others, one by one. In the end, Crane sat there alone, facing the long line of Shad's supporters. It was more than he could take. He faced Shad.

"All right, Wakefield, you may have all of them simpletons fooled, but not me. If you wasn't such a brazen coward, you'd climb off that horse and fight me like a man."

This was what Shad had intended all along. Without a single word, he dismounted. Then, while the others looked on, he unbuckled his gunbelt and handed it to Abe. His hands were still raw from climbing the stone wall, but that was something he'd have to ignore.

Crane was still seated on his horse. He looked at Shad in disbelief, for he never expected him to call his bluff. Now he'd have to make good on his challenge. Everyone was watching him to see what he would do. Still he hesitated.

"Get down from there, Crane!" Shad ordered. "You wanted a fight. You've got one. I've got a score to settle with you."

Only moments before, Crane had been in command. Now, he stood abandoned and alone, looking like a big-mouth coward who wasn't sure what to do next.

"Nobody gives me orders!" he shouted.

"Seems to me that you was the one that issued the invitation," Abe reminded him. "You was the one who called my friend, here, a coward, and we all heard it. Now, it appears to me that you're the one who's acting like a yellow-belly."

That did it. Crane swung his leg over the horse, and as soon as he touched the ground, he took his gun belt off.

"I'll show you who's a yellow-belly," he said.

He rushed forward and swung hard at Shad's jaw. Shad sidestepped the blow, throwing his opponent off balance. Crane turned, and like an angry, raging bull, he put his head down and charged. Imitating a bull-fighter, Shad moved to the right at the last instant, leaving Crane nothing to throw his weight against but thin air. The big man staggered and nearly fell. He was infuriated, now, and he moved in, swinging with both fists. A hard punch connected with Shad's head. It made his ears ring and he tasted blood. Crane followed up with three quick pounding blows to the chest.

"Come on, Wakefield!" he heard from the sidelines. "Give him what-for!"

Shad responded with an uppercut to the jaw that snapped his opponent's head backward. But Crane recovered quickly.

"I'm going to kill you with my bare hands, Wakefield!" he threatened.

Crane was big and heavy, outweighing him by twenty-five or thirty pounds, but with his added bulk he couldn't move as fast, and this was to Shad's advantage.

Crane was coming at him again, with a wild look on his face. Shad feinted and drove a fist into the big man's belly. It shook him, but it wasn't enough to knock him off his feet. Moving quickly, Shad ducked a blow and came in again with a quick succession of punches. Still, Crane was fighting back with everything he had. The big man grabbed Shad and threw him hard to the ground. He landed on his knees, with Crane towering over him. There was no chance to get up. Instead, he drove at his opponent and tackled him, knocking him down. Then he was on top, driving punches into his belly. Suddenly, he felt Crane's hands closing around his throat, and he knew he was only seconds away from unconsciousness and death. With the last of his strength, he rendered a sharp blow to the outlaw's head. It was enough. His opponent went limp, releasing his deadly grip. Shad rolled off and lay gasping for air. Never in his life had the Colorado grassland smelled sweeter. He looked up to see Abe standing over him.

"You done good, son. You done real good."

He was alive. That was all he could think about right then. Slowly, he got to his feet and shook his head to clear it. His body ached and his mouth was bleeding, but he felt exhilarated. Crane was sprawled on the ground, and he was out cold. Shad figured that he'd just settled the score.

"That was a fine show of pugilistic skills, my boy," said a voice that he recognized instantly.

He glanced over to see a patrician-looking man with a gray handlebar mustache. Beside him was a younger man who wore the star of a United States Marshal on his vest.

"How in the world . . . ?" Shad started to ask, for Judge Madison had arrived with the law.

"Oh, we had no trouble finding you at all, young man. The first thing we did was to stop off at the Crane ranch. Hardly anyone was there. But we were told that the boss and the rest of the hands were out tracking down a villain named Wakefield in order to hang him. Seeing as how I'm well-acquainted with the villain, my friend and I decided to track the trackers and get in on the necktie party. Mostly to spoil it, mind you."

"Well, I'm glad to know that you're still on my side," Shad said.

Lucy Craddock must have decided that she'd been ignored long enough. She pranced over to the Judge and the marshal.

"Judge Madison, I'm sure you remember me. We met in Denver City on numerous occasions."

Shad noticed the amused look on the Judge's face.

"Of course, Miss Lucy, how could I forget such a charming young lady?"

He was spreading it on thick for a woman who had no real charm to her name.

"My brother and I are the heirs to my uncle's ranch, and we've had a horrifying time because of an outlaw named Rumbaugh."

Abe decided to put his two cents worth in. "Shad saved her hide," he told the Judge.

They could all tell that she didn't appreciate the intrusion. But the Judge looked pleased.

"Always glad to hear good things about my godson," he said.

Lucy's ears perked up at that revelation.

"But Judge Madison, you said that your godson was a St. Louis lawyer who owns a big cattle ranch near Trinidad."

Shad was keeping an eye on Crane while he listened with interest. He was especially interested in the part about his owning a cattle ranch.

"True enough," the Judge agreed. "Shadrach, here, is a lawyer if he should he ever choose to practice. He also owns a sizeable cattle ranch, should he ever choose to take possession of it."

Shad was startled when Lucy Craddock turned and looked at him like she was seeing him for the first time. All the old hostility was gone, or maybe it was just suppressed.

"How interesting," she said. "I was just about to offer him a job as foreman of my own ranch."

Like sin she was. Until her conversation with the Judge, she'd considered him to be a thirty-dollar-a-month saddle bum that she couldn't get away from fast enough.

The Judge chuckled.

"Miss Lucy, I'm afraid that's a little like offering President Grant a job as groundskeeper of the White House," he said.

This brought another look of irritation to her face that she couldn't hide. Their positions had suddenly changed.

"Now, if you'll excuse us, my dear, I'm afraid we have pressing business to take care of," the Judge went on. "Gentlemen, Marshal Fairchild is here to deputize Shad and the rest of you who rode with him. That way everything becomes nice and legal."

"Isn't it a bit late for that?" Lucy asked with a trace of sarcasm.

"The way I look at it," Marshal Fairchild explained, "is that I was the one who was late, and nobody else should be penalized for that. The deputizing is retroactive. Everything you did this past week, you did as my deputies. Your duty ends as soon as you decide to end it, or the middle of next week, whichever comes first."

Shad noticed that Crane was coming around. Awkwardly, the rancher got to his feet.

"Heard you was trying to have yourself a hanging, Mr. Crane," said Marshal Fairchild.

Shad's former boss was all set to say some strong words to Fairchild, when he noticed the star he was wearing and thought better of it.

"You'd better not try something like that again," the Marshal warned, "or it won't go easy on you."

Crane bit back a reply and turned toward the men who'd worked for him.

"Come on, let's get back to the ranch. You've all got plenty of work to do."

The men looked at Tex, who ended up speaking for them.

"None of us want to work for you anymore, and I doubt if you'll have an easy time finding anyone who will. You see, Crane, none of your hands can ever be sure that you won't take the notion to hang them on some pretext or other."

The humiliations were piling up. He'd just been soundly beaten by a man that he'd called a coward and tried to hang. Then he'd been scolded by a United States Marshal, and now his hands were quitting him.

"Do the rest of you feel that way?" he asked.

"Tex spoke for all of us," one of them assured him.

He walked over to his horse and strapped on his gun. Then he mounted up.

"Don't none of you come around my place begging for a job," he said. "I'm through with the lot of you."

None of them said a word, and Crane rode off alone.

"Any of you that don't have jobs," said the Marshal, "I'm drafting you to take these prisoners to jail. The rest of you can go on your way with my thanks."

With that, Marshal Fairchild and his newly drafted hands rounded up the prisoners and headed out. Kaminski, Trujillo, Loftis, Beale, and Osborn said their good-byes. In spite of his sister's scrutiny, Henry Craddock managed to give Shad a casual salute before he and his sister rode off with the others. That left Mc Nary, Abe, the Judge, and himself.

"You got yourself quite a beating," said Abe, "are you going to be able to ride, son?"

Now that it was over, he was feeling his new bruises, as well as a lot of other aches and pains.

"I can ride," he assured them. "But what's all this I hear about my owning a big cattle ranch. You were stretching it a mite, weren't you, Judge?"

His former guardian laughed.

"Well, maybe I was a little. Your father invested in the ranch years ago, so you're only half owner of the M Bar W."

Shad's mouth fell open in astonishment.

"That's where I worked as a cowhand when I first came back to Colorado. I thought Frederick White was the owner. He was out there all the time nosing around."

"Nope. Fred just had an uppity way of acting like he was the owner. He was, in fact, my assistant. Mc

Nary, here, is the foreman of the M Bar W, now. But you and I are the owners.

"You see, son, when you first got back, you weren't ready to take on that kind of responsibility. But I can see that you've matured a lot. You're a man now. I think you're ready."

A ranch owner. He kind of liked the idea.

"I'm ready," he said. "What do you say we head toward Trinidad?"

They were mounting up when they heard Rumbaugh.

"Hold it!" he ordered. "You're not going anywhere."

The outlaw had made his way down the mountainside, where he'd hidden in the scrub and watched. It was likely he'd witnessed the confrontation and the fight. He'd waited until the others had gone, and now he was holding a gun on them.

"If I was you," said Abe, "I'd have lit out of here while I had the chance. All of them killings you've done is going to get your neck in a noose."

The outlaw was completely clear of his hiding place now, and he'd pulled himself up to his full height.

"Well, you're not me," he said. "I'm going back to my ranch and start over, and nobody's going to say a word against me. Nobody can prove that I broke the law in any way. But Wakefield, here, is going to pay for all the trouble he's caused. Mc Nary is, too, and since I can't leave any more troublesome witnesses, I'm going to get rid of all of you."

Mc Nary's hand started slowly moving toward his .45.

"I wouldn't try that," Rumbaugh warned, and watched as Mc Nary's hand eased back.

While the outlaw was focused on Mc Nary, Shad caught Abe's eye and nodded slightly. Abe understood. He edged over to one side while Shad moved to his left. With the greater distance between them, they were more difficult targets. He saw that the Judge was alert, waiting for a chance to act.

"Get back where you were," Rumbaugh ordered.

They ignored him.

"You see," said the Judge, "we've got nothing to lose, and that's a distinct advantage."

"Shut up you old windbag!" Rumbaugh yelled. "I'm through talking—"

Mc Nary started to rush him and he fired. Mc Nary went down. At the same time, Shad drew his Colt and squeezed off a shot. It hit its target, making a hole in the outlaw's shirt, right at chest level. There was a look of disbelief on Rumbaugh's face as he dropped his weapon and fell.

"That's for Charlie," said Shad, but he doubted if the killer could hear his voice.

Abe and the Judge patched up Mc Nary, who had a nasty side wound but was lucky that the bullet hadn't messed up anything important.

"I'll be okay," he assured them. "I've taken worse than this before."

After Mc Nary had been tended to, Abe and Shad took on the task of burying the outlaw close to where he'd been shot down.

"Want to mark the grave?" asked Abe.

"No. I reckon the man and his burial place is best forgotten."

With the last chore finished, they mounted up.

"Guess it's time I settled down and started looking after my ranch," Shad said.

The Judge chuckled.

"I've been waiting to hear those words for a long time, son. Your father would be proud of you."

With Mc Nary on one side, and Abe and the Judge on the other, Shad Wakefield turned his face toward Trinidad.